Hot Erotic Sex Stories

Swingers, BDSM, Spanking, Gangbangs, Bisexual, BBW Erotica, Lesbian First Time, Medical and Much More

Brad Shepard

Table of Contents

An Unforgettable Trip

They dropped us off with helicopter in the centre of the Atlantic Ocean, sporting speedos and hot bathing suits, and we are awaiting the manager and team to get there. Staring at one another, wading in the seawater miles and kilometres away from any sort of property.

"So what is this film about?"

Inquires the puffy blonde celebrity together with me, within a youngster's floating tube using zebra patterns, attempting to maintain her hair away in your water. Unlike some of these others, I'm at a wetsuit with diving equipment, an air tank. I need to choose the mask and then breathing tubing from my head to react. "Cannot you see the script?"

"I tried," says the girl, her breasts drifting in the water beneath the very small bikini top, "however, it was too perplexing to me."

"Well," I start, "it is around..." My mind draws a blank. "We are in the centre of the sea and..." I do not recall. I swear that I read it only the other night, each line of this. I recall stating: "At last, a porn movie I would be pleased to behave in. So fresh, so revolutionary." However, I do not recall just one phrase from it.

All I understand is that it happens in the centre of the sea. I have to be losing more brain cells than I ever believed.

I simply stare at the blond girl --Jenna; I believe her name is with a dumb/blank appearance. I then turn and float into a different cast member, Randy, the only thing near some buddy in this industry, probably since we have a fascination with AMC cars, notably Matadors. Randy is shutting and opening his own eyes a stunt at the water wings onto his arms to keep him moan.

"Hey Randy, would you own a copy of the script? "Saltwater leaves his eyes plump and also the sunblock on his nose does not appear to be assisting. Turns for me personally,

"No, I've never got you. They said I would get it. As soon as I told them that I got you, they said among the team would provide me with a replica on the helicopter; however, the team was not about the helicopter."

"They're coming by ship."

"Yeah, so I have never seen the script. Can you forget?" "I made it in your home; we seldom comply with the script anyhow." I gaze down to the water to see my flippers waving back and forth, inches beneath my flippers the heavy azure water becomes more shadow.

"It is bugging me. I read the script; however, I cannot recall anything about it. I recall actually enjoying it, even really-really liking it that's all." Randy shrugs his bare shoulders.

"All that I know is it is the largest budget porn movie this business has been ready to test."

Chewing on a pruned finger "And it's shot completely on location in the centre of the sea." Randy turns into the bald girl with a complete match of tattoos, that did not bother to put on a bathing suit since she has one tattooed on her privates. "Shady, have you got a copy of the script?" The bald woman smiles at him always smiling and twitching.

"No, they would not let anybody take it to the helicopter."

She holds her arm up to scrape, tattooed down and up together with sun-faces and dragon scales.

"They did not want them destroyed in the water" Randy calls into the whole cast of porn actors, "Does anybody know exactly what this movie is all about? I had not been provided with a script..." Everybody looks at one another, suspended in question-faces, fighting with ideas.

I really don't believe one of them is able to give us a response. "I understand what it is all about," one of them states, profound voice. Yes, it's King Soul, that the large title of the movie, the elderly well-endowed black celebrity who has been performing these movies for almost twenty decades.

A true professional. Obviously, he probably understands the script, memorized it word for word, the scenes that he does not execute in. He has been proven to deal with porno scripts like he is behaving in a true film, or perhaps even a drama. Most of us swim, circle round the King. He enjoys the attention. Significant smile in his hot water goat beard, scraggly like pubic hair. "So, what is it about?" I inquire.

"Well, it is about a lot of people stranded at the centre of the sea. There is some gender. Parts of this are filmed on a single island. Tons of other bizarre stuff also."

"Kinky material?" Shady asks, bending her palms. "Freaky material?" Jenna appears anxious. "I am... Well..." King Soul starts.

"Well, only odd things. Unusual things. Like those things in art theatres."

"Like what?" I inquire. The King considers this for a moment, hands in his facial hair.

"Not sure," he states, and we groan in reply. "I see it long ago it could all be a memory. I had a few fantasies about the film. Not certain what was that the script what was fantasy today." "I cannot think how disgusting that this really is!" Randy squawks.

"They stated how important it had been for us to really read the script once, but not one of us may recall one detail!"

"Talking of Terrible..."

I say, gently. "Does anybody know if the team will get here?" Our eyes roam to the manager's boat, appearing into the horizons. Nothing, the sea stretches for miles in all directions without a predictable end.

"How are they likely to find people?" Jenna, just like a tiny kid though the earliest girl here. "They asserted that they would not lose me. I am fearful of oceans" "They cannot lose us" King Soul states. He retains a little mechanism such as a walky-talky having a blinking red light onto it. "I had been given this monitoring device.

They know precisely where to find people. They are just late, that is all." You have to look around soul, everybody in the industry does. He is so serene, has everything in check. They say that he graduated from school but did not actually brag about doing it. We all did not even make it through high school. Hell, I just acquired a GED. But he is not the sole one; we appear to Shady too occasionally.

She has been taking art courses at the community school for so long as I could recall. We can relax for today, but my thighs are getting tired out of water that is bottled. I must allow myself to float occasionally to enable the muscles a break. The fantastic thing, most of us have powerful lower bodies out of doing so a number of these movies.

We're all in good shape, old spirit, for this type of legwork. The eleven people hold closely together, keeping each other warm as the wind starts to pick up. We quit speaking to each other if the sun goes down again.

Water smacking from our own bodies at the silent skin moisturizes and moisturizes, hungry. The water starts to get hot about us, hugging us like a mattress. I open my eyes again. I see half of the heavens is murder-black; however, there is a deep blue line on the opposite horizon, sunlight going to produce. I transfer my thighs and my head jerks clear.

I recall where I'm. My lower half numb from the hot water, twisting my bare toes back and forth from the darkened sea. I'm not wearing the wetsuit or diving equipment, but am in a speedo which isn't at mine. Maybe I exchanged costumes with somebody.

I am lying in my back and my top half floating about something tender and comfy. I switch to my left side. Nobody is in this way. I appear to the best. Nobody. I think facing me. I am all alone. I believe something to rub against me beneath the water. Screech and jump, splash from the sea, searching for what'd touched me.

It was a hand, a hand. Jenna. She's floating face down into the ground, still in her drifting tube. I was around her corpse, sleeping her this entire time. Maybe I'm the origin of her drowning.

I do not recall in any way. Shivers crawl my spine as I see her body rocking into the dim light.

"Where's everybody?"

I request the water; however, the water is active whispering to itself. I lift Jenna's head upward. At a delayed burst, then liquid burst pours from her nose and mouth and eyes and ears. I shake at sight, appearing nearer. Her eyes are open, but the eyeballs are overlooking. And there's not anything inside her outside the eyeballs possibly, hollow.

She's empty inside, only a shell full of water. Her skin, about the inside and outside, was shimmering white, her mouth hanging open, oily tongue dangling out. Just like a fish mouth.

"What happened to you?"

I ask. She seems clean. Not horrifying or disfigured, simply clean. Empty and unhappy. I let her slide through the tube and gradually sink to the dark depths, her vacant corpse refilling itself. I take her location at the tube, a pretty tight match, but I will have the ability to endure for quite a while without needing to control water.

The strip of lighting at the horizon isn't growing any larger. The sunlight does not wish to develop. Did everyone drown? Maybe they murdered themselves. It would not have been difficult, take a deep breath of plain water than all of the blacks.

Perhaps they're using Jenna now. However, Jenna. What happened to her? Her insides. simply vanished. Maybe she had some insides. Maybe -- A voice. Somewhere in the space. I am able to listen to it marginally in the shadow.

I cannot find that way. There is a fog in this way. I listen to the voice. A bit more distant. It's true though. I am sure. Definitely, someone is seeking to locate me. Maybe the manager and team have arrived by ship. Or they may have delivered a search party for us.

"Over here," I shout into space. Those assholes. Fucking assholes. They arrived too late. I am the only one left today. Yeah, I suppose I should be glad I am really being rescued, but everybody else is still dead.

"Over here, over here," I shout. I get nearer to the voice, so this becomes nearer to me. However, there are not any ship noises. Only a voice. I understand that it is. Randy. He is still living.

"Randy!" I call. His remote voice develops somewhat louder and louder till we're in a position to grasp each other. Although we're still not able to observe each other at the skies. "What happened?" Randy cries. "I do not recall anything. Can the helicopter wreck?" "Exactly what do you believe?" I inquire.

"The last thing I recall is getting onto a helicopter to film the newest film on an island. I then woke up in the centre of the sea. It frightened the shit out of me. Where do you?" "I am here." His voice is really near me; however, the fog is getting thinner. I cannot view anything.

"Keep talking," he states. "Do not you remember yesterday whatsoever?" I inquire, paddling furiously.

"Yeah, we moved to the pub and purchased an eight-ball."

"That was the day before."

"It had been last night, remember?"

"You have to be delirious,"

I inform him. "Yesterday we had been dropped off at sea. How can you forget? This was the complete catch into the movie. It was likely to be filmed in the centre of the sea. We had been awaiting the manager's ship for here, but they never showed up."

"What exactly are you speaking about?" Randy yells. I believe I could make him out in the space.

"The movie will be a few dumb run-of-the-mill pornos onto a deserted island. It was likely to become a Gilligan's Island parody."

"No it was not, Soul stated it had been an avant-garde porn movie set in the centre of the sea."

"What exactly are you speaking about? That is hopeless. For starters, Americans don't do avant-garde flicks. And how the hell are we all supposed to fuck at the centre of the sea?" My mind gets dizzy.

Can he be confused, or am I the mistaken person? I really don't believe I could think straight. My mind's in pain.

"It does not matter exactly what happened," I inform him. "We are both likely delirious. In any circumstance, we are at a shit of difficulty."

Nonetheless swimming each other; however, we've yet to fulfil. "Have you noticed anybody else?" he asks. "I woke up to Jenna," I inform him.

"She is dead."

"Do you believe anybody else lived?"

"I doubt it. I just recall you and Jenna using things to float.

The remainder of them could have been spilt water all of this time. I really don't believe they left it" "So you believe that they'll find us."

"Not if that insanity does not tidy up, I cannot actually find you", And Randy came to perspective, lying on his back to stay afloat. His water pockets stretched to his / her sides. "That you are," I inform him paddling my toes in his leadership.

His eyes shut. I catch his leg and pull him into me, simply seeing him in his comfy posture. However, he does not finish this comfortable posture.

"Randy..." I hit my hands to his shoulder. "Come on, stop fucking around." And that I jerk him to wake up. A popping sound. Randy opens his eyes along with water stems from their sockets, flowing from his nostrils and mouth. I dab backwards, almost from this tube, laps my arms. Face dunks to the sexy sea. Attempt to regain myself, huffing/choking breaths.

A couple of minutes of all calm-breathing and that I slide the water tails out of Randy let's sink from view.

"You also, Randy," I convey to his shape under me. "You're vacant inside, like Jenna." They shouldn't have had spirits. Only hollow gloomy creatures with no on the interior. I suppose most folks in the adult movie industry are without spirit.

Finally, since I think Jenna once explained, the company squeezes it from you enjoy juice, after which you do not care about anything else anymore. A spoonful of water moves in my lungs, and I cough into awareness.

"Hey, look who's awake," Shady states, splashing water. And that my eyes move in and out to watch her head, and her bald head shining in the dim light.

"Told you he would wake up finally,"

I listen to King Soul from me. I clear my mind and look round. You can find five of these. "What happened?" I inquire.

"The last thing that I recall is locating Randy dead."

"That is all you remember?" Shady asks. "You did not go awry till two weeks after we discovered you. And you also told me you discovered Randy empty that afternoon."

"I really don't remember seeing some of you because of the very first moment. How long are we here?" "How long, Grim?" Shady asks the lanky, bearded biker man to my left hand. "olden times," he states in a female voice. Wait a moment.

"Eleven days" Shouldn't we be dead by now? "The jellyfish are keeping people alive," Shady states. My coughing face lumps into more queries. "You are the person who found them" Grim informs me his face really bisexual in its attributes. "Appearance," Shady states, jerking her monster hand to the ground and pulling a translucent jellyfish as large as a mind, squirrelling in her wrist.

"The very first night we had been out here you touched to the water and then pulled out one."

"There is enough vitamins and nutrients to keep us."

Spirit informs me "But now we are beginning to think they are poisonous, which makes us reduce our memory."

"We have not fed you in a while," Shady provides the curling jellyfish for me personally.

"Eat."

Biting to the live monster, twisting limbs around my head. Water. Cold new water flowed my neck, along with the monster, stops moving.

"It is refreshing water," I state.

"Yeah," Shady informs me.

"Just like a dwelling water balloon" A rubbery exterior with just water indoors.

"There are hundreds of them around us," some woman says.

"However, you cannot find them because they are clear."

Once I chew on its stretchy down meat, I gaze in the water searching for them. However, there's nothing. Only crystal water.

"What happened to the others?" I inquire. King Soul: "You mentioned Jenna and

Randy drowned. Toby and Camesis vanished the very first night just like you. And now, Norma. Well, there has been. a shark that has been following us for the last couple of days. It chose off the weakest people yesterday. You likely would have been following."

"What about the monitoring device?" I inquire. "What monitoring device?"

Shady blinks her eyes that are tattooed.

"Spirit includes a monitoring device," I inform them.

They've confused appearances. King Soul digs into his purse about his shoulder.

"That which I gave me is here," Soul states. "However, I do not recall.

"He is so shocked to find the device on his hands he nearly falls.

"That is it," I state.

"However, it had been uninstalled before."

Soul clicks a button, and the red light starts blinking again. "It had been turned away..."

"We are saved," one of the women says.

"They will find us today!" Shady:

"I hank God, you recalled."

A wave of aid blows them through, but I am surprised they'd forgotten about it. It is something I wouldn't ever let leave my thoughts. "Incidentally, was not there twelve people assumed to be from the film?"

A woman asks. She is the woman who was likely to function with Shady from the sunken underwater scenes.

"Exactly what do you believe?" Shady asks.

"They constantly have twelve cast members in every movie they produce."

"I really don't understand what you are discussing."

"No, that is correct," Soul states.

"They're constantly strict about that. But was not there twelve people fell off from the sea?" "No, you will find eleven people," the woman says.

"Vixen," Shady sets her hands on the woman.

"I believe you are right. Hold on. You will find the six people, Norma, both Randy and Jenna, both Toby and Camesis. That is eleven." "Who was the twelfth?" Vixen asks. Shady:

"You and I will fuck, Randy and Mark will fuck Jenna, Soul was likely to fuck Norma and Camesis, Grim was planning to fuck Toby. Who is left?" The shy woman, a newbie at the company,

"I do not understand who I'm screwing?"

Most of us turn into her, Cyl; I believe her title is. Yeah, pretty certain it is Cyl. A moment of my hand reaches in the atmosphere.

"The small man!" I shout. "Who?" They inquire.

"You know the tiny guy." Disposition:

"Oh yeah, the midget."

"I am putting a midget!"

Cyl shouts.

"Perhaps not a midget,"

I state.

"A tiny individual. Keep in mind he always gets angry once you call him a midget."

"What is it matter?" States Soul.

"Midget is only another term for small."

Vixen: "However, what happened to him?"

"He was not about the scene," Grim says.

"Yeah, he had been," Soul states.

"The whole helicopter ride appears to be a dream today, but I swear that he had been on it"

"Can he get off?" I inquire.

"Yeah," Soul states, "that he was swimming, making us laugh with his suggestions."

Me: "Where's he?"

Disposition: "He should have vanished like others."

"Are you certain you did not dream?"

Vixen asks.

"No," he states.

"Obviously not, I confuse my fantasies with memories."

"I am glad he is dead," Cyl states.

"I do not need to fuck a midget."

"Who was supposed to sleep?" I inquire.

"I told me," Shady states. "You and Randy were likely to perform Jenna."

"No," I inform her.

"You stated Mark and Randy were" They gaze at me personally.

"You're Mark," they state. "No, I am not..." Wait a moment. What's my name? "It is not Mark; it is..." I shake my head. "Mark," Shady sets a dragon arm,

"that is difficult for all."

"My name is not Mark!" I push her off.

"Then what should we call you again?" Shady asks.

"Do not call me " I state, swimming away from her.

I wake up one morning at the wetsuit back, praying I'm not lying on a different dead/empty body. My eyes were looking. I visit King Soul sleeping, Grim holding up him. Cyl sleeping, using Vixen carrying her. And I turn my mind, discovering Shady is supporting me, ensuring I do not drown in my bed.

"You did not sleep," she informs me.

"I really feel as if I have been sleeping," I inform her, rubbing on my eyes using succulent numb fingers.

"You have been awake for days," she informs me" and just slept for one hour."

"How long are we here?" "You have forgotten?" I nod.

"We stopped counting a long time past. Per month or two, possibly."

My eyes burn hot in her voice, wanting to shout. Shady states, "our memories continue moving out and in, particularly if we sleep. We do not understand how honest our memories come."

"I do not recall very much whatsoever."

"Nothing has been really worth remembering. We only take turns eating and sleeping jellyfish daily. And occasionally one of us loses all the memory, and we must clarify a whole lot of things."

"What about the monitoring device?" I inquire. "There is not any monitoring apparatus," Shady states in a voice that is bent.

"What happened to this? Can it break? Sink?" "No," Shady states. Spirit started it. There was nothing within. Only a box with a blinking red light."

"Are you certain?" I inquire. "It was only a prop for the movie," she states. "Not only a true monitoring device."

"Well, everything about the shark?" I inquire.

Shady pauses.

"What Earth?"

"There clearly was a shark they said it murdered Norma."

"No," Shady states. "Norma drowned. There has nothing but jellyfish here."

"They stated it was a large shark which killed her in 1 bite." "Your memory is playing tricks."

A high-pitched shout and everybody jerks vertical. A fin is located at the water violently splashing alongside Cyl. Vixen yanking the young woman from the fin that is straightened.

"A shark" Grim yells and everybody awaken together in a tight ball. The shark fin enhances to the water. Cyl was shrieking on the very top of her throat. We maintain her out of thrashing arms thumping us.

"My toes," she yells.

"View my toes " We pull her to the tube, exposing the shark snack on us. We leap trom her if we view it. Her toes have been missing. But there isn't any blood. Her thighs are hollow, nothing within whatsoever. Water gushes from the holes into the sea. If she sees her thighs, Cyl stops yelling. Like she was not actually in pain. Her eyes fall broad. Simply staring at the flow of water draining from her limbs that are hollow.

"What the hell are you?"

Vixen shouts. The shark is still circling in the background; however, most of our attentions are around Cyl now. Cyl is perplexed, stunned perhaps, maybe not saying a sentence, not breathing. She lifts her wrist into her eyes and examines it carefully.

Subsequently, she pokes a pit using a fingernail. A thin line of water sprays like a pit. Everybody is watching the shark, as she starts to drink out of her arm. She then looks up and smiles.

"I am like the jellyfish," she informs us. And then she drops back, tired.

"I am sexy," she states.

"I am so sexy. The water. "

Shady swims for her, staring into her legs.

"She is right," Shady states.

"She is just like a jellyfish."

All of them sigh, such as the entire puzzle, was solved. Subsequently Shady snacks into her arm, then ripping off the rubbery skin out of her. Cyl does not yell, seeing Shady weigh her just like a jellyfish.

The remainder of them combine, gnawing on Cyl's epidermis, water squirting out to their mouths. I float behind her because Shady chews that the rear of her mind off. She is completely hollow inside. And I will see the rear of your face.

"Stop doing this," Cyl states, and watching her mouth proceed from the interior sends claws in my creaky neck. No vocal cords no mind, no bloodstream. How does she operate?

"She is a jellyfish, Mark," Shady states, stuffing among Cyl's vacant breasts into my mouth.

"Eat."

"Wake up!"

Somebody yells via a megaphone. I open my eyes into a little speedboat facing me. A cam is inserted in my way. My vision clears, and I see three guys standing at the ship. A camera guy, a solid guy, and also the manager together with his megaphone.

"We've got a porno to create," he states.

"no more sleeping at work "

I really don't understand the guy. He's not the manager I recall. In fact, I do not recall at least one of these guys. We have had the exact same manager for many years, we proceed drinking baseball games, but these individuals are absolute strangers, so yelling at me just like a drill sergeant.

I am unsure what the initial team looks like or exactly what they were; however, those folks aren't them I am convinced of it.

"Start fucking," the manager cries.

I visit King Soul and Grim have been double-teaming Vixen around there, lying floating tubes, so fighting to have an adequate position.

I flip about to Shady, that had been cradling me in my bed.

"When did they get here?"

I ask.

"A few days back,"

she whispers.

"They have been working us night and day. I really don't believe we could do it. They will not let us at the ship till they have sufficient good footage for the film."

"Proceed below water" the manager yells, extending his hands like God. Shady and I'm squeezed beneath the ground, jellyfish pulling us down, then curling around our limbs and then sucking on under the ground.

Invisible animals forcing us, my wetsuit rubbing her burst flesh. We utilize my oxygen tank to shoot turns as they pull us to the shadow. They open a pocket at the crotch of the wetsuit, they slip the insides of her thighs, and they then shift us together like puzzle pieces. I see Shady throughout the mask, and her eyes shut tight with dread and perhaps joy, the jellyfish caressing the backs of the thighs and shoulders. However, my thoughts jerks awake as I understand I believe nothing within her. She's hollow/ vacant in there. I am only moving in an open area.

I move softly. I can't continue. Over Shady's shoulders, the shark is slowly coming, diving us to get an assault. I catch her, push our way through the slick jellyfish, her hollow body mild enough to take. We burst throughout the face and Shady requires a deep breath.

"Get back down there," the manager cries at us.

"Shark! Shark!" Shady yells.

Along with the shark jumps from the atmosphere, flying over our minds like its own fins are all wings. Most of us update our eyes once we see that the shark gets pink-peach epidermis and big human-like breasts beneath it.

Plus, it lands around the Grim, that was hard at work involving Vixen's legs before it came on top of him. The shark starts squirming along with him. It's screwing him. He yells at us to get assistance, but we can't move.

He attempts to shout; however, the shark bites right into his head, tears his mouth off. Water gushes from Grim's head; his mind is hollow inside. His lower head lost, Grim's eyes appear around, seeing the shark/woman because she rapes him.

"Keep moving! This is excellent!" The manager yells, cheering to the shark.

"That is what we've been waiting for!" Vixen is trapped under Grim. King Soul gradually churns off without needing to provide help. Vixen pushing Grim however they're hooked with the floating tube along with the weight of this shark. Jerking arms punches, however, the shark won't quit fucking Grim and starts to consume more of his beef, yanking his arms out of the sockets and then slurping down them, hammering the remainder of his mind, sucking his torso as she squeezes her shark-breasts around him.

"Oh, what a film!" Screams the manager. Vixen strikes the shark trying to eliminate, along with the shark slides at her, shooting her whole face away, along with the shark continues its rampage around Grim's lesser half. Faceless Vixen swimming away.

"Mark," the manager yells, "go fuck the shark at the buttocks!"

"My name is not Mark," I reply, swimming off in your rapist fish. In a safe distance, I flip to watch Shady and also King Soul slipping onto the speedboat. The manager cries to come back to have sex with all the shark. Soul, in their predator speedo, has a sharp object in his hands.

A knife possibly, or a broken beer bottle, something he discovered him closes on the ship. And since the sound guy turns to him, Soul slashes him half, his entire body cut into two, fold backwards, empty interior. Water splashes in Soul, blinding him because the director and camera guy turn into a strike. Vixen's faceless body is swimming at my way, after my splashes. I try dismissing her, the horrifying appearance of a woman swimming and living without the front of her mind.

I see Shady from the water. Her tattoos are like fish scales covering her skin, fighting the manager together with all the boom rack, in her nudity, however together with her examples, she never actually looks nude.

She is a beautiful lady, though a porn actor. But she is empty inside today; all her attractiveness is simply on the exterior. She punches the pole through the manager's torso; however, the manager proceeds to swing the megaphone in her. King Soul cuts on the camera guy's leg away, water draining into the ship. Vixen, the creature, is supporting me today. She grabs me and keeps me caressing my flesh.

The shark jumps to the ship, tearing to the camera guy, and it's torn in half longways. His water drains from him, but one half is still standing. One leg and one arm, balancing. The sounds of this shark ingestion rubbery meat.

Tonight's left half remains vertical long enough to reduce on the boss's head away, leaning to one side and popping his mind straight from its neck, either of them crashing to the water. Shady standing in the ship: Her head features a bewildered look as if waking to the situation with no memory of it happening. She jerks if she finds the shark at the ship, fucking and eating a guy.

And she shrieks if she sees Soul's correct half sitting at the ship, wiggling in her. One by one, then she tosses the guys to the water, along with the shark chases after them. I attempt crying at Shady; however, she does not appear to listen to me.

She has to be horribly perplexed. And Vixen keeps me tight in position, won't allow me to float into her, wrap her thighs around me. Shady turns about the ship and rates to space, the shark after near. And I am lonely in the sea again. Alone with Vixen, the abomination. She's still caressing my entire body.

I look in the rear part of her mind because she doesn't have eyes to check into. She moves my hand round my skull to pull me closer to kiss her again. But with no mouth, my head slides right into her bare mind and kisses the interiors. The rear wall of her mind is salty and slick. I shut my eyes, holding her closely in the water.

I wake up on a shore, staring up in glowing sunshine. Salt-foamy water simmering me around. I sit. My garments are white tuxedo. My head feels equally like white, such as a blank piece of paper. The island is lush with vegetation and mountains, a flow of water leaking out of my nose. Walking up the shore, sunlight after me just like a camera. Just like I'm a T.V. show to sunlight. Following a long time, I find a dining table with two chairs.

A piece of white fabric was covering it, using a centrepiece of wildflowers. I sit in one of those seats, cleaning the sand from my tuxedo and palms. My face enters the tablecloth eyes drifting. "Could I get you something, monsieur?"

A scratchy voice inquires me. I lift my head and watch just a tiny guy of three and a half feet standing on a log and also sporting a white tuxedo virtually equal to mine. In addition, he wears a fitting eye patch.

"Excuse me?" My thoughts are spinning.

"Could I take your order, monsieur?" I look in my palms since if a menu then looks back at the tiny guy, my mouth agape, squinting my eyes. "Yeah," I inform him. "Give me the roast beef."

"Really good, monsieur," says the tiny guy, writing it down in a laptop computer.

"What will you enjoy as a drink?"

"Just water," I inform him.

"Really good, monsieur," he states, scribbling words from his laptop computer.

"Are you encounter somebody, monsieur? Or dining?"

"I do not understand," I inform him. There's a girl, In my opinion, striding across the shore. She sees me and waves, grinning wide. I don't understand her, but she appears to comprehend me. The girl is naked but includes a white gown tattooed for her entire body. Her mind is hairless of hair has a white dinner coat tattoo, then tilted to one side. The grin grows even larger once she sits in the tiny table from me, stating,

"Hi, Charles, is not it a fantastic day now?"

"Yes," I state, half-smiling straight back to her.

"Among the finest I have seen."

Her eyesight decreases to my hands along with her grin turns angry, stunned.

"Oh, my God! Your ring is twisted!"

She rips my hands from its resting position and corrects a wedding band that's been in my finger. Subsequently, she holds our palms together and that I see she's an identical ring tattooed on her finger.

Once she determines her ring is lined up with hers, then she pops up her face into my sight also brings her back a very big grin.

"Your water, monsieur," the small guy says as he pops a sandy glass onto the desk. And the tiny guy closes his good eye and puts his hands in his mouth, biting off it in the suggestion. He then fills my glass with all the water from within him. I sigh as I have a drink, my hands prisoner to the girl's grip, attempting to pull away from it. The little man scurries for her,

"And to get madame?" As I gaze in the space to get yet another happy couple on the shore.

A girl overlooking the front of her mind, burying half a black guy from the shore soil, along with the wave flows without the permission of the moon.

First Time BDSM

Cindy had read stories and seen porn showing BDSM relationships and the thought of rough sex had always turned her on, but she never thought these types of relationships were real...or that she would find herself in one and so deeply in love with her Master.

Cindy was your ordinary working mom and wife. She had met the love of her life and they had three amazing kids together. She was normally open and honest with her husband about her fantasies, but kept parts of herself hidden deep inside out of fear. Fear of rejection, fear or past abuse, and fear of the unknown. One particular steamy night, Cindy admitted to her husband that she wanted to watch him have sex with another woman and hear him tell her that she's better than Cindy. The idea of it was enough to cause Cindy to cum instantly.

The next day, Cindy's husband decided to open about his secret desires. He let her know that he wants a slave girl. One he can tie down and have his way with, whip and spank her, give her orders outside of just sex and she complies. Everything Cindy had read about but never been brave enough to purse. She couldn't believe what she was hearing. It was everything she wanted finally presented to her and all she had to do was accept it. Cindy told her husband she would try to give him what he asked for, but to be patient with her as she learned to please him. She began calling him Master at all times and learned to please him in ways she never imagined.

One day at work, Cindy was extremely busy and hadn't been able to perform any of her assigned tasks or even respond to her Master. It was starting to get late and she knew she would need to leave the office soon so she could still make Master his dinner. She started packing her items up when she heard someone walking towards her desk. Cindy looked up and Master was walking towards her with a very frustrated disapproving look on his face.

"You haven't spoken to me today slave girl. Have you completed your assignments?"

Cindy was embarrassed to have him belittle her in the office, but answered honestly.

"No Master. I'm sorry, I have been busy."

"I don't want excuses slave girl. You know you are to let me know when you are going to be unable to complete your tasks and you choose not to. For this, you must be punished."

Cindy didn't know what to say or what to do. How could he embarrass her in her work place? And how could she show her face around her coworkers tomorrow if anyone were to see or overhear this?

"Yes Master. I am sorry. I was just packing up to head home. Thank you for taking the time to decide on a punishment for tonight."

"No girl. You misunderstand. You will receive your punishment here. Now. Time to strip off your clothes and on your knees in front of me."

Cindy was terrified. If she did as she was told and anyone saw, she would lose her job. She had put her soul into her career for the last few years and couldn't imagine losing it anymore. But if she were to disobey her Master, her punishment would be worse and he would force her to complete it here anyway. She she obeyed, removed her pants and shirt and dropped to her knees.

"No slave girl. I don't have patience to explain this all to you. Remove all your clothing and bend across your desk for spankings for not obeying this simple order."

Cindy stood back up. She removed her heels, stockings, panties, and bra. She leaned across her desk as ordered and awaited her spankings.

"I'm going to give you 10 spankings for disobeying. Then you will get on your knees and prepare yourself for your next order. Count with me slave girl."

"One" she said. Whack! It came hard, hot, and fast. Cindy knew these would welt and fast. "Two" she cried. On and on until she had reached her 10. "Thank you Master." She whispered, afraid if she spoke any louder she would start sobbing.

She dropped to her knees as ordered and dropped her face to the floor in a sign of respect for the man she loved so much.

"Good girl. Now, we are putting your leach and collar one. You will then walk me around your office and show me where your time was spent today. I want to see what has made it so hard for you to inform me of your day."

"Yes Sir" Cindy said to the floor. She secretly hoped no one was in the office and the cameras weren't on. She would be humiliated and surly would lose her job for this. She felt Master place her thick black collar on her and remove her elegant day collar. She then heard the clip from her cold metal leash being snapped on to her collar. She did as ordered and stood completely naked except for her collar and walked Master to each meeting room that she had spent time in today. With each stop, she would explain to her Master who she meet with and why the meeting was necessary for that day. She could see the understanding start to play on Master's face and hoped the punishment was coming to a close. The last stop was one she was hoping to avoid. For a few minutes after her last meeting, she had stopped by David's (her desktop support person) desk to joke a bit and blow off some steam. Cindy was afraid to tell Master about this as she could have gone back to her desk and text Master.

"Through her Master. After my last meeting, I stopped by Desktop and spoke with David." To Cindy's horror, she could hear typing coming from the area they were walking towards. She started to slow down and look back at Master.

"Walk slave girl. We will see where you have been."

Cindy turned the corner to see David was still in the office and completing some work. David looked up and saw Cindy completely naked being walked around the building on a leash.

"Um...hi Cindy. Everything okay?" David said, not sure what was going on or if he should even acknowledge her.

"Hello David. This is my Master, Johnathan. We are walking through my day." Cindy's voice was barely a whisper. She had turned dark red, mortified that David was seeing her nude and on a leash.

"Hello David. I understand Cindy stopped by here this afternoon. Was something broken?" Master said, enjoying the fact that Cindy was struggling to fight the urge to hide her body from David's eyes. He was going to keep this conversation going for a bit longer.

"Um, hi Johnathan. No, nothing was broken. Cindy stops by every day to joke around for a few minutes to break up the work day. She came over and we talked about the awful music playing as background noise in the meeting rooms. No disrespect here, but if we are going to talk, I need Cindy to put her clothes back on. I can't think with her naked in front of me."

Master could see it wasn't embarrassment that made David request clothing. It was clear he was attracted to Cindy and wanted to do more than just look at her body. This gave Master a devilish idea.

"David, are you almost finished with your work? Cindy has been disobedient today and I'm trying to punish her accordingly. I think you might be able to assist me, if you are willing."

David looked confused, but intrigued. Cindy look horrified. She didn't know what Master was thinking, but inviting David to join in with any part of her punishment made her terrified and started to moisten her groin.

"I'm finishing up now. Just need to clock out and then I'm up for anything. What do you have in mind?"

"You know where Cindy's desk is. Meet us there after you clock out and we'll see a fitting punishment for her." Johnathan smiled and pulled Cindy's leash to lead her away before she could protest.

Cindy walked silently back to her desk, afraid to protest as this would earn her a slap across the face. Or worse, Johnathan would take it as she's not ready for this relationship and end everything they had been working to achieve. They arrived back at her desk and Master surprised her by pulling out rope he must have stashed on the desk next to hers while she was unaware he was there.

"Now, slave girl, I'm going to tie you down to your desk and your friend David and I are going to have our way with you. You will do as you are told by either of us and you will not orgasm here. Do you understand me?"

"Yes Master. But..." Cindy began to protest to having David touch her, but she was cut off by a quick backhand to her mouth.

"I didn't ask your feelings for this slave. I asked if you understood." Master yelled at her. Cindy could feel herself become wet after Master raised his voice and punished her. She knew this is what she wanted and willfully submit to his orders.

"Good girl, now place your wrists together and extend them so I can tie you down."

Cindy extended her arms and felt the familiar loving embrace of the rope on her wrists. This was one of Cindy's favorite items Master would use. Being restrained sent a thrill through her body and her mind. Master placed her on top of her desk and tied her hands above her head and legs down and spread wide. Some time during the set up, David had appeared and couldn't contain his excitement

"I get to touch her? However I want? And she can't move or object?" He asked.

"That is correct David. I will allow you to do anything you want to her tonight." Johnathan responded with a smile on his face.

Cindy was dripping wet already. She kept her eyes closed because she felt like she was dreaming and didn't want to wake up. She didn't speak out of fear she would be hit again. She just prepared her mind for what was about to happen.

"Turn your head towards me and open your mouth whore." She heard David order. She did as she was told and began to suck his hard cock. She noticed David wasn't as thick or as long as her Master, but he would do just fine. She continued to suck as he slowly fucked her mouth. She felt the unmistakable tongue of her Master invade her clit. Master knew she would be on the edge of an orgasm quickly with the current arrangements. It never took her long if she was sucking a cock while her pussy was played with. Cindy felt rough fingers on her tits. She could not tell if these were Master's or David's and she dared not look. She could feel her orgasm getting close and began to moan in her throat and knew David could feel it in his cock.

"Remember slave girl, you will not get off tonight. If you disobey, you will walk home completely naked for the world to see. Do you understand?" Master spoke while barely removing his face from her pussy.

"Mmhmm." was all she could muster as she was fighting the urge to cum. Master stood and slapped Cindy's pussy to help calm her growing need. David could not believe his luck at joining this fuck session and was nearing his first orgasm.

"I'm going to cum on your tits whore. You don't deserve to taste my full load." David pulled his cock out of Cindy's mouth and jerked himself to finish on her tits. She could feel the hot load land and smear across her chest. She started to feel frustrated as she wanted to cum for them.

She felt the head of a cock near her mouth. She opened without waiting for an order, knowing this is what was expected of her. She knew the familiar smooth skin and taste of Master's cock. He pulled it from her mouth and slapped her face with it.

"Stupid slut, no one ordered you to begin sucking nor did you ask permission to taste me." Cindy felt ashamed. She knew she was to ask for Master's cock. She was too caught up in this experience and was forgetting her place as his slave.

"I'm sorry Master. Thank you for correcting me. May I please have your cock in my mouth?" Cindy asked, louder than was needed but wanted to assure Master that she would work harder to remember her place.

"Good girl. Yes, you may suck my cock now. And David here is going to push into your pussy. Remember, do not orgasm." Master sounded amused which made Cindy smile. She took Master back in her mouth and felt him start to fuck her face. He pushed in deep and caused her to choke multiple times, but she loved trying to deep throat Master and please him better. David began fucking her pussy, fast and hard. Cindy couldn't believe how great it felt to have two cocks in her and know her holes were pleasing two men. She loved feeling used and dirty.

Master soon reached his climax and also refused to cum in her mouth. He pulled out and jerked off into her hair. She then heard Master fumbling around, looking for something.

"Master, can I assist you with something?" Cindy asked, knowing he would have to untie her for assistance, but she asked out of habit.

"No slave girl. David and I are looking for our phones. You look too good with cum on your tits and in your hair. We want pictures of the little office slut full of cum and tied to a desk begging to be fucked." Master said with a smile playing into his words. He loved taking pictures of his used slave and showing them off to his buddies.

"I will print these off and post them all over the office if you tell anyone about us fucking whore. This will be our secret." David chimed in. Hearing the dominance and authority in his voice just pushed Cindy even closer to orgasm. She knew she would go home looking like a used slut tonight. Master began to speak again and it took Cindy a few moments to realize what he was saying was about to happen.

"Now slave girl. I'm going to untie your arms from the desk and loosen your legs. I'm going to slide under you and fuck the ass that belongs to me. Do you understand?"

"Yes Master. I understand." Cindy repeated out of habit. Master has taken her ass multiple times before and was prepared to have him again. She felt her arms release and noticed her wrists were still bound. She felt her legs release just enough to lift her legs to the desktop and prop herself up so Master could slide under her. She loved the feel of his warm skin against her and could hear him breathless in her ear.

"Now girl, I did not bring any lube so you are going to take me and feel every pound in your ass. There is no backing out of this." Master breathed to her.

"Yes Sir." She was trembling. She didn't know if it was from fighting her orgasm for so long or if it was from the fear of being fucked in the ass with no lube. Either way, she was going to do as Master instructed. She felt Master push slowly into her ass. Thankfully, by this point, he wasn't looking to punish and hurt her. Just to finish himself again. After a few moments, he slide further and she could feel the entirety of his hard cock in her ass. It hurt badly and she wasn't sure she could really handle it, but Cindy was determined to try. Just then, she realized David was still there. Would he fuck her mouth again? Would he just jack himself while watching? Soon she realized it would be neither. He pushed his cock deep in her pussy as Master thrust again into her ass. Cindy couldn't believe the pain and pleasure she was feeling. Double penetration was something she had always wanted and had tried with Master and a dildo, but nothing could prepare her for the real thing. She knew she would not be able to control her orgasm if this continued. She shuttered hard against Master and heard him chuckle in her ear.

"Yes girl, you are being fucked in every hole tonight. You have pleased me tonight be being brave and honest. For this, I will allow you to cum once. You will hold off until David reaches his orgasm and then you will let go and cum hard for us. Do you understand slave?" Master said loud enough for both of them to hear.

Cindy was panting hard and started sobbing. She could not believe that Master would reward her with two cocks and was going to let her orgasm. "Yes Master. Thank you Master. I will not disappoint you." She felt Master and David fuck her, their pounding almost synchronized inside her and brought her to the edge of an orgasm.

"Master! David! I'm going to cum! Please, please cum in me!" Cindy screamed. She didn't care anymore if there was anyone left in the office. All she cared about was cumming with the two cocks currently pounding her drenched pussy and torn ass.

"One moment slave girl. You need to know something. I've been talking with another whore. Tomorrow night we're going to meet her for dinner and I'm going to fuck her in our bed. I've seen her pussy. She's tighter than you. I can't wait to feel a pussy worth fucking." Cindy couldn't take it, she gushed at this moment and came hard against David. Luckily, David had reached his orgasm and came with her, deep in her pussy. Johnathan loved that he could push his slave to this limit and came in her tight little ass.

Slowly, they all stood and dressed in silence, not sure what to say to each other. Awkwardly, David shook Johnathan's hand and thanked him for the fun time.

"Any time David. You are welcome to use my slave in the office whenever you see fit. You may fuck her mouth or her pussy whenever you decide, but don't enter her ass. That is my area." Johnathan said. Cindy couldn't look David in the eye, but could feel the excitement to know David would be using her again.

"Come slave girl. It is time to go home and feed your Master."

Cindy obeyed and followed Johnathan downstairs. She sat in the car quietly and reflected on the happenings for that night, bewildered and excited by what just took place. Finally, she spoke to her Master.

"Sir, if I may. You said we are meeting another woman tomorrow and I will be watching you fuck her. Is this something you said to get me off tonight or is this really happening?" Cindy wasn't sure if she was excited or nervous for the answer, but she knew she needed to hear it.

"Oh, my sweet little slave girl. When do I ever lie to you? I don't need tricks to make you orgasm. We will be meeting for dinner at 7 tomorrow night." Was all he said for the rest of the drive...

Darrion's big black cock

Life wasn't the same for Donna once she had tasted Darrion's big black cock. Darrion had enkindled the slut sleeping inside her and Donna couldn't believe the transformations she went through. Gone were the days of Orthodox, conservative ideas, Donna had shaken off her traditional and orthodox dressing ideas that used to hide her lush seduction under expensive fabrics from lecherous eyes. She now preferred mini-skirts, jeans, and micro mini skirts. She was liberated to wear sexy tops, even if she wore a gown, it would be too revealing to flaunt her seductive assets and cleavage. Men would drool and strive hard to keep their jaws from falling onto the ground to witness such a sexy slut walking just beside her husband. "Is that a pimp waiting to share his wife? What's on the table baby?" How many times Donna had heard those vile comments passed behind her back. The more she heard, the more her arousal and excitement grew to be a complete slut.

Gary was happy for his wife in a certain way. Before Darrion moved into the neighborhood, Donna used to stay at home. She hardly would attend any parties or visit any rock music festival in the county. Her outing included her daily sunbathing, and weekend visits to the local culinary restaurant to have some mouth-watering dishes. But since Darrion entered her life, Gary was amazed to witness the transformation of his wife. The way she talked, the way her aggression grew, the extent to which her confidence about sex grew, the way she carried herself and the level to which her introvert qualities diminished was amazing and breath-taking for Gary. With a sexy wife by her side all the time, Gary found his interest in sexual and animating bedtime pleasures. His wife's breath-taking blowing capacity, performing ministrations on his shrimp penis, keeping him on the edge all the time, riding his shrimp dick to the extent of passing some degrading comment was too stimulating and arousing for him. And he was happy for his wife. And too naïve to consider his wife was all his after her sultry transformation.

But Donna to some extent had stopped cherishing sex with her husband. She found it funny to an extent how her husband's shrimp dick vanished in between her juicy udders if she thought to give him a boob job, or how his small penis would seem like a peanut in her mouth compared to the chocolate bar of Darrion. Yet she decided to hide her true self from her husband. She was never in the choice to harm his pride or demean him in public. But her frustration grew the week Darrion went for a week long vacation. Donna couldn't find Darrion in his house. She tried to reach his cell phone, but that was unreachable. Darrion wasn't there to train in the yard with his dumbbells, Donna was missing the mesmerizing sight of a true black Hercules flexing his appeal to tempt and corrupt her mind. Darrion wasn't there to teach her any sex lesson, oh she missed that dearly. Donna was going crazy. She desperately tried to feel the true joy of the highest heaven during sex with her husband, but she found that very underwhelming and immensely depressing. It wasn't Gary's fault. He was a healthy man, in every way and he was eager to satisfy his wife as well. But, her husband's shrimp dick wasn't capable at all of getting hammered and stuffed in all her holes like a bitch in heat. Donna was desperate to feel another big black cock inside her, shoving the pits of her married womanhood, making her feel like a woman she was meant to be. Darrion was well aware of that and he just lusted to starve his bitch.

After fifteen days, Darrion returned to the neighborhood. Seeing her black stud at the door brought back lustful savage memories back to her mind. Donna felt her pussy on fire and her knees weakening. She embraced him in her soft, cozy arms, kissed her hand and lips desperately. She fell to her knees instantly and said, "Please" as she kissed the black Hercules's crotch over his jeans.

"Bitch," said Darrion perusing her shorts, "Did you miss me. You're the only thing in this shithole worth anything. If I can't have you, at that point I'll just have to hang tight for fat Gary to return home. I should kick his lazy ass. You're one hot bitch in town. You're my bitch."

"Please don't hurt my husband. He's so nice to me." Donna stated.

"Just in that event he can't stop me from feeding his wife's married holes with my juices. Then he's dead meat. Oh, fucking Jesus! I missed you my slut!" Darrion asserted.

Donna leaped back as the black man's huge hands had unknowingly bounced up as if to squeeze her succulent tits. She had already known the power of black studs and that thought shot chills down her spine trembling her a bit. She had realized that black men were sex-starved animals, particularly for White, Hispanic, and Latina girls. Donna hoped that her body would be sufficiently provocative for Darrion after so many days.

"I have been dying to see you Darrion, I missed your lessons," Donna gulped at her own savage statements.

Darrion just nodded gazing in stun at her tits. As an after idea, Donna teased, "Do you have any more lessons for me, Darrion?"

"Uh, sure baby, but you haft do what I tell you." Darrion asserted.

"Like what?" Donna asked curiously.

"Like to begin, I'd like to see you out of those shorts." Darrion snickered.

"Alright," said Donna. She felt her heart pounding like a thousand drums at the idea of sucking a black man off, but she would say the more stirred she made him, the greater would be her pleasures of the highest heavens. She turned around on her feet and bent down to touch her toes, her bare succulent bosoms were visible between her legs to the black stud. The word BITCH was gazing at him as she reached up and gradually pulled the legs of her shorts down.

"Your ass is fucking mind blowing," said Darrion massaging his groin. "Now take off the thong." He reached out, caressed and finally squeezed hard her two ass cheeks.

"Shit," she thought. Her heart skipped a bit and she trembled like a leaf in a whirlwind as he was going to run his strong black hands all over her body again; she was going to fly the zeniths of sexual pleasures with her lover again. Donna was breathing intensely as she ventured forward. She shivered with savage excitement as he leaned forward and kissed her tummy, slipping his tongue inside her belly button. He strongly grabbed her hips to keep her still and kissed up her stomach. Donna's lush body responded with goosebumps coursing all throughout her radiant skin from his wet kisses, and that wrecked havoc when he reached her juicy bosoms. They'd generally been excessively sensitive to his touch. Darrion's tongue slid up her lower bosom, and over her nipple, sending electric pulses through her body. The thick tongue returned, this time orbiting her nipple before he sucked the whole tip between his lips. Donna sucked her bottom lip into her mouth to keep from screaming out in delight. A groan escaped her lips as his teeth delicately closed on her nipple and nibbled on it. Darrion at that point sucked it like an infant for a few minutes before kissing his way over to her other bosom.

This time it was somewhat unique. Darrion's mouth still gave her nipple an exercise, but now his hands were also progressively attacking her body. He slid his one hand slid along her thigh and gradually went in between her legs. It climbed to her groin and ventured into her ass, grabbing the thong. Darrion gradually pulled the thong down, utilizing his other hand to pull the straps over her hips. His finger hooked the thong descending from her ass. The tips of his finger pushed more diligently against her anal cavity, making her bounce, but didn't infiltrate. Rather, it continued descending. The tip slid over her pussy lips, which a lot to Donna's surprise were exceptionally wet, separating easily welcoming his finger.

Darrion's finger pushed against the passage to her pussy but propped up until it was teasing her clit. Donna hadn't been touched, ravished suddenly and teased like this in quite a while and she was battling not to scream out loud. Gary did his best to please her, but his inexperience was too absolute to train him up. Her body was battling the electric stimulations. Her clit was swollen as his wet finger teased around it. His finger at that point slid between her pussy lips once more. Darrion thrust his finger somewhere deep down in her pussy just as he sucked her left nipple hard between his lips. "Oh! my fucking god," groaned Donna as she came all over his finger.

Darrion was exceptionally skilled with his finger. He didn't stop subsequent to giving her the one climax. He held his finger in deep and began pivoting the tip around while proceeding to suck on her juicy tits. Darrion was a Hercules and his finger was almost the size of Gary's penis. Donna shut her eyes and appreciated the sensations. The black man's free hand came up and crushed her ass cheek, one finger near her anal cavity. This time he pushed the finger hard against her asshole. Donna opened her eyes in sheer shock of the excitements as his finger pushed in, she was about to say something, but found that she was getting cum for the second time.

Donna's legs went weak as the enormous climax wracked her body. It had been almost two weeks since she experienced such an intense orgasm, and never twice within minutes and never one this enormous and certainly not while with Gary. Darrion immediately grabbed her waist and brought her down to the ground as she crumbled to her knees between his legs. The moment had finally arrived for her 'please' to be fulfilled. She should appreciate it. Darrion too flopped on a couch.

The curvaceous, black-haired, once upon a time faithful and conservative wife laid her head on his knees while regaining her composure. "I'll take that blowjob now," he commanded.

Donna gazed up and Darrion was unbuckling his belt and opening his jeans. He took off his tee-shirt uncovering his muscular, strong chest. Darrion had the chest of an expert weightlifter and he put Gary to disgrace with his enormous brawny figure. There was additionally an enormous lump underneath his pants.

Donna reached up for his zipper. Her fingertips were freezing with stirring excitement. Her mind was corrupted with savage lust. Darrion might have been black, yet he was an attractive masculine man. She believed she expected to repay him for the two climaxes she'd had. Donna got her hands on the zipper carefully and started to drag down. The lump underneath his pants appeared to swell, the additional pressure, helping to drive the zipper down. Darrion lifted his hips while she helped pull his jeans down. She was going to witness the man's penis who taught her the art of seduction and she was beginning to get somewhat excited.

Darrion wore tight white briefs that showed up going to blast. It nearly appeared as though he had pushed a big black mamba in his pants. Donna could see a serpentine head moving. Donna sensed her hands were shaking as she grabbed the rim of his briefs and pulled out. That was only the open door the snake had been searching for and Darrion's cockhead shot up not only past his briefs but past his belly button. Donna gazed at Darrion's monster penis and she continued gazing mouth agape in stun. "This was the tool that I had been dying to drill myself on to," her mind screamed.

Darrion's hand descended and pushed his boxers free of his nut sack. "Seeing it will not make it cum, bitch. Slurp on it with that pretty tongue and lips of yours." Darrion twisted his mammoth cock forward and laid it on Donna's lips.

His voice brought Donna out of her stun. Darrion's pole which was indeed thirteen and a half inches in length and as thick as a big mag flashlight. "Oh! I missed them," she muttered as she took in balls the size of tangerines. Darrion appeared to be considerably greater as he pushed it down and she gazed intently at his big black pole. He held his cock bent as Donna kissed and licked around the golf ball-sized head.

Darrion let go of his enormous black cock and the shaft sprang up to slap against his belly. Donna reached up and grabbed it, pulling it back towards her mouth. Donna paused, gulped somewhat in savage lust and somewhat in shame. She was behaving like a cheap roadside slut as if she were anxious to suck on this hunk man's big black cock. She pulled her head back and gazed at it some more. The swollen head was light brown while the pole and the rest of Darrion's body were pitch-black. A pulsating blue-black vein ran the length of his pole and smaller veins crisscrossed the surface. The Herculean man's enormous cock started getting nearer to her mouth again and Donna abruptly felt Darrion's hand on the back of her head, dragging her forward. She surrendered and opened her mouth.

At some point during the blowjob, Donna started to have fun. When considered, it was very quick. She brought the bulbous cock head into her mouth and nimbly ran her tongue all around the surface. Her other hand found the pole and began stroking it. Donna had thought she was talented, but that was sucking on Gary's prick. And she had to practice a lot to regain her grades while blowing this muscular stud. Her husband's whole penis had easily fitted into her mouth with simply the tip teasing her throat. Donna felt again like choking with simply Darrion's cockhead in her mouth. Sucking Darrion was a test and she cherished the challenges.

Donna forced the thick cock into her throat and began bobbing her head. Donna's throat made purring sounds as she took the cock deeper and deeper. Her luscious lips and soft tongue felt like heaven to Darrion, she was slurping on the big black cock lubricating it efficiently with her saliva. "I think you missed this fuck meat slut, don't you?" Darrion teased. Donna gave him a mean look, but continued bobbing her head. "Not as simple as little old fat Gary, is it? But I hope you did a lot of practice on him." Darrion asserted.

Donna gasped for air. Darrion was enjoying his married slut's ordeal on his giant cock after so many days. His slut was relishing the exquisite sultry experience. That's what she missed with her lovely and sweet husband. "Just tell me when you're going to cum," she said before restoring her mouth to his pole. The base had developed smoothly now, well lubricated by her saliva, and her hand slid faster along it while she'd figured out how to swallow eight or ten inches. Her free hand hefted and caressed his balls which were beginning to contract. The thick shaft was expanding considerably thicker. It yanked in her mouth and Donna felt it siphoning semen into her belly. Confused and somewhat horrified, she pulled back as a greater amount of the hot liquid shot down her throat.

"I'm going to cum," moaned Darrion, excessively late.

Donna's mouth was loaded up with hot sperm and the bulbous cock head kept her from letting it out, forcing her to swallow. The black mamba was hosing into her throat, choking her and feeding the hot protein juice. It was too much for her. So, Donna pulled back liberating the cock from her mouth and soon it blew another wad that splattered from her nose to her neck. Donna pulled the spitting head down away from her face and a few additional wads covered her tits. Donna moved his cockhead around, utilizing it to rub his semen into her skin and nipple. "It is so white, so rich!" she mumbled somewhat stunned. Her chin and breasts were covered with milky white sperm, so different from Gary's. It even tasted unique, more exquisite, more potent, filled with protein. "God, I missed this taste so much," Donna thought inwardly. Darrion's rich juice resembled eggnog compared to Gary's skim milk.

"You seem a lot out of practice. You should have swallowed all of it," Darrion winked.

Donna felt herself moistening at her yearning pussy, "Yeah, you know my husband is no match for you."

"I need to check that sweet married hole of yours." Darrion teased.

"Oh." Donna hadn't released his pole. She was all the while stroking on it, awed that sperm would even now spill out of the head each time her hand moved forward along the big black pole. It had just contracted an inch and was still hard enough to fuck.

"Let me taste that married pit of yours. I would take it as my payment," Darrion asserted.

"Oh, Darrion..." Donna yanked her head back as Darrion's cock pushed forward through her hand, once again rock hard.

Darrion's cock appeared to be increasingly keen on sex. His big black mamba was throbbing harder than before yearning to enter into its most desired pit. Donna also needed to realize and relish the feeling of his enormous dick in her married hole.

"Oh! Let's do it Darrion before my banker hubby returns."

"Alright. But first, we should ensure that you're well lubricated." Darrion laid down on his back on the floor. "Come here, baby." Donna made to straddle his waist, but Darrion stopped her. "No, no babe. Lie over my chest facing the other way." He waited until she had obeyed him and then concluded, "Now back your pussy into my mouth." A perfect 69 position.

Donna felt her already moistened pussy get somewhat wetter at his words. Gary hadn't gone down on her in the past week and she'd cherished more of his tongue than his penis. Darrion grabbed her fleshy ass cheeks and spread them wide as she backed into his tongue. When it came, Donna almost bounced off his chest. Darrion missed her pussy altogether and his tongue licked her butt hole. She was thankful, she'd showered before he had shown up. Darrion twirled his tongue around her anal cavity before moving it down to her labia and sending a shudder of electrifying delight up her spine. His tongue, then slid back up to her butt hole, and then down to her pussy. Donna started preferring having her ass licked nearly as much as her pussy. At long last, he quit licking all over and just worked his tongue into the folds of her juicy and leaking pussy. Donna ended up bumping back into his rigid and straightened tongue sucking her clit and pussy. Darrion's finger gradually pushed into her butt hole and Donna sensed herself to come once more. Nor did Darrion let up, he proceeded to consistently tongue fuck her. Donna grabbed the enormous black cock right in front of her and began kissing and licking all over once again as a way of expressing profound gratitude. Minutes later to telling Darrion, "Holy shit, this is insane," Donna ended up sucking Darrion's cock again as another climax build up. This was unimaginable. Donna had gone a very long time without a climax and was going to have her third one in an hour. Soon her cum was pouring down Darrion's chin.

"I think you're all set," said Darrion, pushing the depleted lady up off him.

Still somewhat dazed, Donna drove herself to her feet. She looked down and saw Darrion grab the base of his cock and hold it straight up needing her to mount him.

Donna turned around and positioned herself over his big black cock. She squatted until the bulbous cock head slid between her thighs. Donna felt his enormous cock head press against her labia, pushing it in until her pussy lips separated around it. Her pussy extended all the way open until the head slipped inside. "Jesus, I missed it dearly. Just the head is tearing me in two," wheezed Donna.

Darrion pushed his hands up to her knees and began scouring them affectionately. "Tell me something, babe, when you expel a band-aid, do you rip it or do you gradually pull it off?"

"What?" Donna inquired. What the hell he would be discussing? She was trying to fuck him and he was getting some information about the bandages.

"You heard me. Do you rip off a band-aid or do you delay the agony by gradually pulling it up." Darrion teased.

Donna thought for a minute. "I rip it off, to get the agony over with as fast as possible."

"Clever girl," said Darrion pushing hard against her knees.

Donna felt her legs shoot back. "Oh my God," she cried as his cock speared her. Darrion kicked his hips and Donna skipped up practically flying off his cock, but rather pummeling down more enthusiastically into it. "Oh, my God! I missed it so much...Aaargh." Donna bounced up again and descended. Each time forced more cock somewhere deep inside her married hole. "No, can't take it. Please stop Darrion... You're too big." Her pussy molded itself and extended around his giant shaft. She felt completely full but was utterly stunned at every extra inch working into her pussy. "Oh god, I love your big black cock." Her pussy descended hitting his groin. Donna had now taken the whole monstrous shaft. "Oh fuck, it's huge. Oh fuck. Fuck! Fuck me like a slut! Oh my god, I love it. Fuck me with that huge dick."

"You like that big black cock far better than your banker hubby's shrimp dick, don't cha?" Darrion kicked his hips hard.

"God yes," cried Donna flying upwards and having a climax as she impaled herself once more. "It's never felt this great. Fuck my pussy. You own my pussy." Donna bounced up and down shoving the big black mamba persistently. She sensed Darrion had stopped kicking his hips and was lying still, but she was the one who was still going on riding him. Her legs had taken over doing everything practically. She got cum on every third bounce or fourth bounce. Donna could hardly focus on all the ecstatic joy she was receiving, but one idea did cross into her mind. It was her most fertile time. "Darrion," she panted, "whatever you do, don't cum in my pussy."

"You'd better slow down then." Darrion asserted.

Donna eased back her pace and the delight was just increasingly exceptional. She could focus on each inch shoving in and out of her married hole. She arched her back and began pinching and squeezing her nipples while sucking her lower lip in. "Sooo big, sooo great," she groaned. Donna felt a major climax developing just as Darrion began working his hips again to get the speed. He inclined up to grab her hips and kept her still while bucking his groin. Darrion snarled so uproariously it frightened her. All of a sudden, her pussy felt soaked. "No," she cried acknowledging his cum. The streams of semen assaulted her womb setting off the greatest climax of the day. She collapsed onto Darrion's chest with his cock still pumping her brimming with seed. Donna recovered just as Darrion's limp cock thudded out of her overflowing pussy discharging a torrent of sperm. "Oh, Darrion! Why didn't you pull out?" She murmured, kissing his chest.

"Relax baby, I've had a vasectomy," Darrion lied. "We can fuck anytime you want, and you won't get pregnant." Darrion determined that he needed to keep this pussy. This hick town wouldn't stand for a wedded White lady giving birth to a black baby. They'd leave town together soon after Donna would deliver.

Donna was feeling somewhat pitiful. She nearly wished Darrion had knocked her up, she was even envisioning there was a warm sparkle originating from her womb as though she had been impregnated. "Wow, our baby would be so ravishing," she imagined how their children would look like. Donna looked at the clock. "Shit," she cried bouncing up. "Gary will be home at any moment." Donna's thighs made squishing sounds as she hurried to the bathroom.

When Donna felt presentable, she ran naked out to the living room and slipped into her attractive outfit back on. Darrion was gone. She opened the trailer entryway to see the huge black man conversing with her husband, Gary. The two men bid byes and Gary moved towards her. Donna could smell beer on his breath. "Darrion said he was giving you company. I love the way you have adapted in the neighborhood." He kissed her lips.

"Oh, thank you, love. I also think as if I have so much to do for the black community and all the communities in this town." Donna greeted him with a kiss, but on his cheeks.

"What a shit? Is he too naive to understand what we two might have been doing there?" Donna felt inwardly.

My Hottest Day Ever

When Brooke can no longer take her sweltering townhouse, she places a call to the air conditioning repair place. While she makes a run to the grocery store for ice cream, the repairman arrives. She was expecting the older overweight balding guy with the sagging jeans, but instead she opens her door to find a tall muscled young man eager to get to work. He soon learns the advantage of an experienced woman, and she rediscovers the advantages of youth.

I kicked the window unit and yelled another string of cuss words at the nonfunctioning appliance. It was mid-August and I was sweating up a storm. Not only had my main air conditioning stopped working, but now my back up system, the window unit, had also died. It may have been 88 degrees outside but inside it felt closer to 800 degrees.

I had already stripped down to a tiny little tank top and cut off shorts, and was tempted to lose the rest of my clothing except for the fact that the repairman would be there in a few hours. I was not sure I would survive until he got here, but I guess I had no choice.

My townhouse was nice. I had decorated it myself after my divorce and was very pleased with the outcome. I had been sorely tempted to just rent forever so that I did not have to worry about things such as the air conditioning, but I guess regardless, I would have to face these things. At least when I owned the place, I could get faster service than waiting on the maintenance guy from the complex to stop by, tell me the air conditioner is broken, and then he would call for the repair guy and I could wait indefinitely. As the homeowner, I think I got higher priority.

Anyway, so here I am sweltering away in my townhouse waiting on the repair guy. I am not looking forward to the visit. These guys are usually around fifty and overweight with pants that sag in the back when they bend over. Not attractive when you are already in a bad mood!

I am so glad that children have not entered my life just yet. That would just be unbelievable to deal with at this point. I am enjoying my single life immensely, and have no plans to settle back down in the near future. Sure, I am on the backside of forty, but I still look damn good for my age. I take care of myself at the gym, and for the most part, I make the right decisions about what I eat. And I do still get the drooling stares whenever my friends and I frequent the bars. But overall, I do not have a significant other. I'm significant to myself!

I decided to run to the store while I wait. It is only up the street and the company has my cell phone number should they need to reach me during the ten minutes I will be gone. I may just go hide in one of the freezer cabinets but we will see when I get there.

I did not even bother to put on more clothing; I just grabbed my purse and cranked the A/C on in the car while I drove. I did not end up climbing into the freezer section, but I did hold the door open longer than necessary while I was choosing my flavor of ice cream. I ended up with the same one I pick every time, but I like to browse. I grabbed the mint chocolate chip and clutched it to my chest as I carried it to the checkout counter.

I guess I did not look too bad, even in my state, because the young man at the register was definitely raking his eyes over my figure. I grinned at him and placed the ice cream down, not realizing until it was too late that the cold container had caused my nipples to tighten up under the thin cotton tank top.

I blushed slightly and tried to slide behind the credit card machine in an effort to maintain some dignity. It was too late, the teenager was already grinning goofily. I paid for my ice cream and made a quick exit to the car. By the time I got home, there was a repair van parking outside my unit and I breathed a sigh of relief as I pulled into the garage.

I hurried around to the front door and whipped it open, still clutching the bag with the ice cream. I almost dropped my frozen treat when I found myself staring at a well-built young man. He had to be several inches over six feet tall, not quite thirty with curly dark hair and sparkling brown eyes. His white muscle shirt clung perfectly to his damp skin so that it outlined his flat pecs and his bulging biceps. His jeans were just loose enough to sit low on his hip bones. And while he looked a little nervous, he did seem to be looking back at me with the same appreciation so I grinned and held up the grocery sack.

"Ice cream? It's a little warm outside, and even warmer in here."

"Ms. Andrews?" he stammered.

"Oh, you can call me Brooke."

"Oh, ok. Brooke, I'm here about the air conditioning?"

"Well come on in before the ice cream and I both melt right here!" I laughed and stepped aside.

When he brushed past me, he smelled of ivory soap and fresh cut grass. I felt a warm thread tickle its way through my lower belly and I shivered slightly as I watched the muscles of his back bunch and twitch as he carried his tool box.

"I'm just going to stick this in the freezer, I'll be right back."

I sauntered off to the kitchen, making sure to put an extra little wiggle in my slim hips.

I returned quickly, offering him a cold bottle of water as I twisted the top off of my bottle.

"Thank you ma'am," he smiled sheepishly.

"Oh don't start ma'am-ing me. I'm not that old yet!" I chuckled.

He nodded, "Got it. Brooke."

"Unit is this way," I pointed down the hall to the utility closet, "and I would love it if you could take a look at my window unit while you're here."

As he followed me hurriedly, I could feel his eyes on the swell of my ass since the shorts barely covered the curves. I bent over more than necessary to unlock the utility closet and I could have sworn I heard him inhale sharply as I did.

****

I took my sweet time, slightly swaying my hips back and forth in front of him. When I finally got the door unlocked and turned around with a proud flourish, I found him shuffling anxiously and trying to look casual as he stared at the carpet.

"There you go, all open and ready," I smiled at the nervous young man.

The little hallway was narrow and I made only the slightest effort to move out of his way, and he ended up grazing my full perky breasts with the side of his arm as he squeezed past me. The nervous young man looked appropriately embarrassed but all it did for me was increase the temptation for more teasing.

As he bent over the air conditioning unit, I admired the firmness of his round little ass before I pressed tightly to his side as though I was actually interested in this antique piece of broken machinery. As my breasts crushed against his bicep, I heard him inhale sharply and I grinned to myself.

"By the way," I whispered in his ear, "I didn't catch your name."

He twitched as my breath tickled his skin, "Andy, ma'am."

"Now what did I tell you about calling me ma'am?"

I straightened up quickly, making my breasts bounce under my thin tank top and put my hands on my hips. He looked up at me and happened to be exactly at eye level with the swells of my cleavage.

He stared and stuttered, "Sorry. Brooke."

"That's better, Andy." I cocked one hip out and smiled at him.

"So what seems to be the problem with this old thing?" I asked as though I would understand his answer.

"I think it's just out of Freon. I have some in my van." He had stood upright and was trying to stare over my shoulder to avoid looking at what I was so clearly offering him, but his eyes kept drifting down to the curve of my cleavage.

I nodded, "Sounds good. I'll be right here."

He scurried off to collect whatever it was he had just mentioned. I dashed to the kitchen and snatched an ice cube from the freezer. I ran it over my flushed skin, leaving my collarbone glistening with moisture and my nipples taut under my thin cotton top. I was becoming more and more convinced that I had to seduce this young man.

When he came back, I thought at first he was going to drop the sloshing container. He gathered his focus and continued toward the hall closet. I grinned and followed him again, running the ice cube over my cleavage until it melted completely.

It seemed a simple job of just filling some part of the air conditioning unit with the liquid. He was finished in short order, and was able to crank the infernal device back on.

"You seem a little warm. Can I offer you some of that ice cream I just picked up?"

He paused and gave me a long hard look. I leaned back against the door frame, making sure all of my curves were revealed through my skimpy clothing. My breasts were thrust out with their perky nipples clearly visible, my waist nice and trim, and the shorts barely covered my ass. I was angled just perfectly for him to see every last inch of damp skin in my hot townhouse. His eyes moved slowly from my neck, over my collarbone, down my breasts and stomach, and then all the way down my legs to my pink toenails.

Andy shoved his hands into his jeans pockets, causing them to sink lower on his slim hips. The tee shirt was now untucked and I could just barely see the hint of his defined abs peeking out. The shirt still clung to the flat hard planes of his chest and his biceps still threatened to split his sleeves in two. The entire scene made me want to run my tongue over the definition of every muscle.

He cocked his head to the side and finally grinned at me.

"Sure thing, ma'am." He emphasized the word ma'am.

I crossed my arms over my chest, accentuating my generous cleavage even further, and feigned anger.

"Now Andy, we talked about that. Bad boys don't get ice cream you know."

He took a step closer and crossed his arms over his own chest.

"What do bad boys get instead?"

I wagged my finger at him and chuckled, "Now there's the question of the hour."

He flashed me a cocky grin and closed the gap between us.

"Maybe we can save the ice cream…" he whispered, only inches from my face.

My heart raced at the nearness of this sexy young man and the fact that he seemed willing to play whatever game I had started made my body tingle for his touch. I rested my palm against his pec and looked up at him. His body was firm and warm under my hand and I fought the urge to touch more of him.

"Are you old enough to handle me, Andy?" my voice sounded throaty to my own ears.

"Are you young enough to handle me, Brooke?" he retorted.

I burst out laughing at his brilliant response, and he cut my laughter short with a rough demanding kiss, pulling my hips firmly to his swelling cock. I moaned softly and threaded one arm around his neck as I gyrated against him.

****

I slipped my hand down between our bodies and slowly ran my nails up the fly of his jeans. Andy's body shivered at the light tease so I kept at it. I tickled and kneaded him through his clothing until the poor boy was panting hard enough to break the kiss.

"Geezus," he breathed, taking a step back, "you're gonna give me a heart attack or something."

I grinned, "There is something to be said for experience, you know."

He laughed, "So I'm learning."

I winked and cocked my head to the side, "You want to challenge young blood against experience?"

"What do you mean?"

"I mean, I wonder if your muscular young body can withstand the tormenting of an experienced woman?"

His desire for sexual pleasure outweighed his good sense and he nodded eagerly.

"Whatever you can dish out, I can take."

I grinned because he had no idea just how devilish I could be.

"What are the stakes?" he asked, looking a little nervous.

"Thirty minutes of whatever I want to do and you do not cum. If you do cum before the timer goes off, you will be my naked handyman every Saturday for a month."

He barked a surprised laugh, "Wow! Ok then. And what if I make it the thirty minutes?"

I knew he wouldn't make it so I offered a similar prize, "Then I'll be your naked maid every Saturday for a month."

His eyes drank in my luscious curves and he nodded as eagerly as a little boy at Christmas. I led him by the hand to the couch and pushed him down firmly.

"Wait here," I instructed him and dashed off to the kitchen for the timer.

When I returned I set it for thirty minutes and grinned at him like a wolf who had found her first baby bunny.

"Anything I want to do?" I double-checked, just to make everything seem fair.

He nodded again, "Anything."

I hooked my fingers into the hem of my tank top and slowly pulled it over my head. I felt my breasts bounce free of the garment and I heard him gasp already. I started to get excited at the prospect of my naked handyman. I leaned over and brushed my nipples against his lips and pulled back just as he parted them to taste.

I slowly started to unzip my cutoff denim shorts and just as the top of my G-string peeked out, I turned around to finish. By the time the shorts and G-string were around my ankles, I was bent over, giving him a perfect view of the firm curves of my ass and just a glimpse of my pussy.

I whirled back around to face him and slowly straddled his lap, rolling my hips against the bulge that was already pressing against the inside of his fly. He moaned softly and slowly moved his hands to my hips.

"Uh, uh, uh, no touching. Sit on your hands," I ordered him.

He groaned but did as he was told.

I laughed, "C'mon, if you start touching, you'll lose the game for yourself before I have a chance to have any fun."

His cheeks flushed pink and he nodded.

I kept grinding and rubbing myself against him until I could wait no longer to see what I was feeling underneath me. I slid my body down against his until I was kneeling between his parted thighs, and I unfastened the button and slowly unzipped his fly. He squirmed at the tiny vibrations it sent rippling through his cock.

As soon as the zipper had cleared his cock, it bobbed out to greet me. He was long and thick and hard already. And he wasn't wearing underwear! No wonder I couldn't see the waistband when his jeans rode low on his hips!

I tickled his shaft with my fingernails again, letting them drift slowly up and down, dancing back and forth. He grunted and tried to thrust upwards but I pulled away so that he did not get the satisfaction of a good hard stroke.

When he sat still again, I reached underneath him and tickled his sensitive balls. They felt weighty and full against my fingers.

"Hmm, how long has it been?" I mused out loud.

"Huh? What?" he mumbled, completely distracted by the sensations on his aching parts.

"How long have you been storing this up?" I bounced them lightly in my palm.

He looked sheepish, "A few days. I haven't had a chance to um, you know…"

"To what?" I fluttered my eyelashes at him innocently.

"You know… jerk off."

"Ohhh, so no girlfriend in the picture?"

"No ma'am," he admitted.

"Now I told you not to call me that," I warned him, "this time there is a penalty for it. You were warned."

I released his aching balls and reached behind me to add five minutes to the timer.

"Ah c'mon," he whined.

"You've been warned young man, and now there is a penalty to disobeying. Five extra minutes to our game."

His cock bobbed at me in mid-air and I wrapped my fingers around the base. He groaned for me and tried to stroke himself with my hand by using his hips. I loosened my grip so that all he got was a light little tickle stroke.

"Fuck," he breathed.

"Give up yet?" I winked at him as I ran my tongue up the throbbing shaft.

He pounded the couch with his fist and shook his head, "No, fuck, no."

Just as he managed to collect himself, I enveloped his entire cock with my mouth and stroked downwards with my lips.

"Ohhh damn…." he groaned loudly.

With my fingers rolling and massaging his full balls, I sucked and stroked his cock with my mouth. My tongue danced lightly over the sensitive ridges until he was panting in time with my strokes. I pulled off to give him a break, and just wrapped my lips around the head. My tongue flicked against that most sensitive spot just under the tip while I sucked and his head fell back.

I suddenly released him and sat up straighter. With his cock slick from my mouth, I guided the length between my full breasts and stroked him with my cleavage. His eyes flew open to watch as the head peeked out again and again, over the top of my tits. Every time it poked out, I flicked my tongue over it.

Out of the corner of my eye, I checked on the timer. I still had fifteen minutes left; I had this in the bag. I released his cock from my tits and buried it in my mouth. With my hand and mouth moving in unison as one long tight wet tunnel, I stroked him. My other hand rolled and tickled his balls until his hips could not sit still.

I slid my mouth down the underside to the base of his cock and slowly ran my lips over the tight skin that covered his aching sack. He was hot and damp as I sucked them each in turn, letting my tongue flick and tickle lightly until his hips bucked hard.

I loosely draped my fingers around his cock again and looked him dead in the eye while I stroked lightly.

"Well big boy, what do we think of experience over youth?"

He panted and stared at me wild-eyed and pleading, "Oh fuck."

I wrapped my mouth around the head of his throbbing cock and stroked him hard and fast, jerking him off quickly as my lips and tongue urged his climax forward. I saw his balls tighten up towards his body and felt his cock surge thicker. I pulled my mouth off just in time and as I stroked his thick hard cock, he growled and painted my tits with white jets of cum. As his body rigidly shuddered against me, I stroked him thoroughly, squeezing firmly to make sure I milked out every drop. He finally collapsed backwards, his limp cock sliding from my grasp.

His eyes slid over to the timer to find that there were still ten minutes remaining. Even without the penalty I inflicted, he would have lost.

"Fuck," he swore with a goofy grin.

"Your punishment starts now, Andy. As my new naked handyman, you have your first task."

"Wh-What's that?"

"To give as good as you got."

I rose off the floor, and lay back on the couch with my own thighs spread.

"Give me just a minute," he chuckled.

"Oh no, no need to wait. Your tongue is nicely warmed up I think."

He grinned and fell to his knees between my smooth tanned thighs. His nails raked up my skin until I could feel his warm breath against my wet pussy. He kissed his way over my mound and down my inner thighs, giving just a little of the teasing I had subjected him too. I suppose it was only fair but after playing with him for so long, I was ready for my own satisfaction.

He finally grazed my pussy with his mouth and my eyes fell shut. When his tongue parted my outer lips and found the hard little button waiting for him, I groaned and buried my hand in his disheveled hair. His tongue drew fast circles and flicked back and forth. He slid two fingers inside my tight wetness just as he caught my clit in his lips. As his fingers curled and his tongue flicked, I cried out and came as the stars in my eyes exploded. He eased me down slowly and finally fell forward, resting his forehead on my thigh.

"At least you can give as good as you get," I giggled.

"Now that I know I can deliver," he lightly swatted the side of my ass.

The air conditioning was back on in force and I felt the cool air chilling my damp skin.

"So, how about that ice cream?" I offered.

He laughed in return, "Sure. I forgot all about it."

"Next time I may choose to lick mine off your body," I hinted.

"Bring it on," he boasted.

I returned from the kitchen, still naked, with two bowls and two spoons.

"You sure?" I challenged him.

I yanked his tee shirt up and found his muscles to be even more lick-able in full view. I dripped just a few drops of melted ice cream onto his defined abs and he squealed. I licked them off slowly and could see his cock starting to swell again. I kept dripping and licking, watching him buck from the cold and then squirm from my tongue. I dropped the cold liquid lower and lower until my mouth just barely grazed the side of his cock when I licked them off. Within just a few moments, he was surging again. Ah, the advantages of the younger man...

I set the bowls aside, and made quick work of removing the rest of his clothing. He whipped his tee shirt off and shifted on the couch until I was able to slide his jeans off completely. With a grin, I climbed on top of him and straddled his lap.

I teased him just a little, stroking him lightly with my fingers until he was rock hard and nudging at my wet pussy. I eased down the length of him, and we both groaned at the snug fit. I paused just a moment to let my body adjust to his sizeable girth but his eagerness did not allow me to wait long. He was soon thrusting urgently with his hips and it spurred my body on. I dug my nails into his shoulders for balance as my stiff nipples grazed his chest. His hands dug into the smoothness of my **ass** as he repeatedly pulled me down on top of his cock.

"Oh God," he groaned, his eyes rolling back in his head.

I slowed my speed and slid slowly, letting my entire pussy stroke and caress him.

"Fuck," he blurted out and tried to pump faster.

I felt the heat building in my lower belly and my toes started tingling as he stretched me in ways I had not felt in years. As his fingers rolled and pulled my aching nipples, the heat exploded and I came as my pussy clenched his cock.

He dug his fingers into the couch until I was finished and then flashed an urgent plea at me with his eyes. I slipped off him quickly, and pumped my hand over his throbbing cock until he again painted my tits and my stomach with his white creamy jets.

As he panted for breath, I slipped delicately off to the kitchen to clean up and returned with two bottles of water and a great big grin.

"So, next Saturday good for you, my naked handyman?"

He nodded, "I'll need that long to recover."

I laughed as the cool air wafted over our damp skin. It was so nice to have air conditioning again that we just laid there naked for the rest of the afternoon.

****

That afternoon, Andy did eventually get around to fixing my window unit as well after a nice cooling off period on the couch. And we ordered in pizza for dinner that night. He did follow through with his promise of being a naked handyman every Saturday for a month. On the last Saturday of the month, I challenged him to another contest and I won yet again. He succumbed to my striptease and blowjob in less than twenty minutes. After two months of Saturday nakedness, we started officially dating and he became my full-time handyman. He is planning to move in with me in the near future, but we have not made specific plans.

He still loves to make bets with me, but he almost always loses. I guess he likes walking around my townhouse naked while I tease and harass him. By the end of his visit, his cock is always hard and bobbing in the air. And I am more than happy to take care of it for him. But I do get a little housework out of it! I'm trying to remember the last time he won a bet between us, and I honestly don't know. Maybe he just likes me getting him off as quick as I can. But he is always the gentleman, and returns the favor.

As we've gotten to know each other, it turns out that he is a sweet young man in addition to his beautiful muscles and loveable cock. Sometimes he will fix an entire picnic and surprise me, or I will take us out to dinner. Someday he even wants to start his own business as a handyman instead of working for someone else.

Don't get me wrong, I'm totally supportive of that goal, but I'll admit that I did give him a hard time when he first told me. Something about horny ladies in hot houses… He just laughed, threw me over his shoulder, and carried me off to bed.

I was not looking for a relationship when I called the air conditioning repair company, but we never know what will fall into our laps. Or more specifically, whose lap we will fall onto!

The Sexual Fantasies

The airline jet engines rattled the takeoff, and Richard Hart felt the sick feeling in his stomach as United Takeoff 793 starts to take it off with a lumbering initiation. He was pressed back into his seat by the heaviness of the forward momentum, and as on each of the many fights he took each year, he recalled that the two most challenging combat factors were the first two minutes at takeoff and the last two minutes at landing... Then he held his breath then clenched his ears hard to open, even though the wheels had not crossed the runway yet. The runway's height and bumpiness were unnerving and the plane spun abruptly and with a hop, he realized he was airborne!

Silently he remembered his song... Swallow, and draw... And he has added a third on this flight... Recall where I'm headed... And why, then!

Jocelyn Haynes, you know. As if the word was in itself a tranquilizer... Or maybe a stimulant that supplanted all his other senses and gave him momentary concentration. His DFW flight to Amsterdam would have been just over an hour... Wait an hour... And marveling at responses, Does she wants to be there? Would she be so anxious, that at the last minute she could change her mind? Maybe as she kissed her husband that morning, he'd caved in on the idea and confessed and begged his forgiveness for the mad folly they'd been infected with for the last few months.

In the management training lecture, the Meeting Richard remembered his first glimpse of Jocelyn... A fresh idea session to encourage tired sales managers to "talk out the side of the box." The young woman with the most beautiful smile and the pales blue gray eyes he had ever seen was what he recalled as he met at the table with those allocated by members of other businesses... They were the color of deep-water pools and he was immediately lost in them. He grinned and introduced him to the group's five other participants, who were to be their team at work.

She accommodates her room so he would join the group next to her and he was glad to be there for the remainder of the day. She was sharp and inventive, with a marvelous sense of humour. He might be assertive but she was very respectful of the group's views... And very quickly a collaborative partnership was established, seeking feedback between them on opinions and ideas.

She looked beautiful... Polished offering evidence of her presence with confidence, but no artificial "glitter" She was wearing a business pantsuit that complimented her figure and well accentuated her rear, She unbuttoned her blouse's top two buttons, and seemed to love the mystery of a strong hint of cleavage... Catching us with a sly wink and a smile... Not the look of "come and take me" but the look of "I saw you staring" and "I like to make you look red."

The four other team members went off at lunch with their box lunches delivered and we didn't spend the day looking for places to escape the conference... So Jocelyn and I just came back from work and sat down to eat our lunches and chat... Discovering that we had much in common and that we both seemed to be enjoying our company, She was my junior for 25 years, but other than the denial of desire (she would never pay an older man serious attention)... We interacted and they formed a growing connection in training.

At the end of the training on the first day, others screamed... "Who is up for drinks" and staring at me, Jocelyn was a question mark. I shook my head, and was saying... "I'm on a hike... Those cobwebs needed to be cleaned out" When I got out of the chair, I found that she hadn't actually approached the crowd at the bar so I asked, "Care to accompany me for a stroll around the premises? "The comment came with the grin light and the twinkle of her eyes.

The meeting join was on a campus of the mid-western university and our rooms were a part of dorms transformed to visitors like us. We strolled around the campus to see the undergraduates and chat about college, life... Relationships, and... Yet we both find ourselves managing difficult domestic situations... Another Common Point: We walked around and we talked... And stopped sitting on the park bench and the conversation stopped having a point and started to exist only for the sheer pleasure of having something which gave valuable time to be around each other.

Supper was the most fun excursion into the student union with the most inedible food in plastic containers but we could barely enjoy it because of the laughter... The feeling was really relaxed and we just seemed to be two more graduates... Yet older and better dressed than the rest of the crowd who fell in their quarters and ate the egg salad sandwiches in the plastic boxes dispensed by a computer with its glittering food server cylinders which looked more like a grip over the '50s. It was like a magical time machine and we had avoided real-life obligations and accountabilities for a moment.

We walked around the duck pond, as the campus was shaded by darkness... And the mood changed... We walked close by and she never stopped when I would slowly push her back with a hand. We stood at the rail and, in the coolness of the evening, I sensed her longing for the comfort of my presence.

My mind was wheeling around... Wondering what her closeness meant, and unsure that it meant anything at all, Wanting to keep the fire flowing I put my arm around her, but not knowing whether that was insensitive and forward. I asked if she was cold and she said "Yeah", and I pulled her in and we both leaned against the rail with my arms brushing outside her... And tasting the blood... And to get overwhelmed by a woman's perfume that near.

My cheek moved close to her ear while I whispered to her, spoke about the ducks on the pond, and wondered about which of the couples might be lovers.

I may had thought I was dreaming but no I am not, we myself and Jocelyn are in Amsterdam to clear our head so we were told as managers, so as to be effective

My emotions switched to overdrive.... To be so loyal to her...... But not knowing if she was friendly to a beautiful older man... Or maybe just something more, I was still trying to figure out where I was... And it seemed awkward so she thought. At last, I said, "Can I go back to your room? "And she said,' Yeah,' with a beautiful dreamy grin. She let me hold her hand back in her room, and she paused at the threshold, and asked... "I had the feeling that you were trying to ask a question at the pond? "I blushed and said" I don't know whether this was a challenge or a dilemma's resolution? "Oh, oh? "Tell me your problem," she answered? "I began and stopped, stammering... And then he breathed deeply... "O... That is the way it is... I was weighing actions which could potentially create problems in a great new friendship with one hand... Over against thinking why I didn't, I'd ever excuse myself that I didn't pursue it. "She grinned blushly... "But what? Have you decided? "I said," Not really... "with my voice shaking, and she smiled sweetly and said... "Isn't it good that we've got two more days to work on your problem solving? "I just had the courage to say in a second... "Anything I want to ask? "Yes, right? "She said drawing herself into the potential of an unwelcome question and steeling it in.

With a nervous cough I asked...... "My goodnight now and may I kiss you? "And we both smiled at the first teenage kiss remembrances. She didn't answer, but with an enticing look on her face, she grinned and went on.

I moved back... Trying not to stick my lounge in her mouth and her lips slid over mine with a peck more like kissing Aunt Martha than a.... What? What? A boyfriend? Hardly fitting for just the brief moments we shared... A mother... A mother... And I did not even allow myself to stay in a semblance of control, thinking and hope.

They stood frozen in place for a moment and she whispered the line from the Jack Nicholson script... "I hope if we try again I can do that better" and our lips met with moist delight... No lips but a kiss that looked like my life's precious breath was sucked out of my mouth.

I looked at her face warmly to assess her reaction... And that beaming smile was there and it whispered softly... "I am going to see you in the morning! "I walked back to my room, torn between the euphoria of" puppy love "and the fact that I had been married to one woman with two grown children for twenty-eight years. Finally, I told myself that she was a very nice young lady who sympathized with an older man... And if I won't want to get frustrated with myself, I'd probably keep the reigns on my libido.

I stepped into the conference room the next day not knowing exactly what I would expect... Only to be met with a dazzling smile and with those blue eyes that give me all their attention. "Have you done really well? "She asked with a smile......

"Having problems last night with his vision... Difficult to tell the truth of fantasies" "Wow, "she said," couldn't you say if you'd kissed or just imagined that you'd? "And then a more profound voice... "I also had the same question" she winked and giggled.

I found the words in one brave moment to ask, "Are they dreaming?..... Or to fantasy? "And she blushed, and gave me a twisted face to know I was put in my spot... But with a smile to know it was a soft reprimand.

The day when agonizing moments are quick. We worked together but just rubbing her arm as we spoke or her shoulder was so easy when we bent over the table to formulate a strategy. I was glad that by pairing, we didn't disturb the group's "decorum.".. Yet I wanted to hold her in at the end of the day.

When the demand for drinks came as a leave time from the others, I asked, "What about silence for a good supper somewhere... Don't believe I'm supposed to serve you egg salad tonight again? "She smiled and the tension that had taken us all day with it began to relax and we went shopping for a restaurant... One with a quiet atmosphere and a private dining room. We stood in whispering holding hands and laughing, and not being as hungry as we would be... Not for that which was on the table at least.

I knew we needed to talk to end the meal... Then I say, "Have we got to talk about that kiss? "Her eyes looked down and there was silence for a long moment... And she said calmly, "I know you're married... And I am anything but... Six years of marriage and life together counts pretty well. "I responded softly," I know. "She said simply," I don't know what I mean... I really liked this kiss... And I adore you...

I'm not looking in my life for a new romance, or an end to the current one... What's up with you?

"I breathed deeply, and said," I know how you feel... I know it's crazy and it's definitely stupid to see this as something more. I have sources from which I don't want to take the... Yet "with a long sigh and a pause," my heart beats like a child, my mouth is dry... And the most thrilling experience of the last twenty years is I expect will happen to me... Last night I'm all about you and I can't keep my hands from touching you now... You corrupted me and some of me would go insane if all we shared were just the kiss! "In a sharp breathless voice, Jocelyn asked," What do you want Richard to do? "I shut my eyes and tried breathing... Wanting to respond with all the emotion it did, but frightened to threaten her with the bluntness.

"You should tell me Richard" she whispered.

"Jocelyn, I like you" I stammered.

After a long pause, the tension increased... It was clear that she was grappling with her response, just as I had my question.

"And Richard... What are you talking about? "I closed my eyes for a moment, not wanting to look at her, and with the excitement I was creating with my voice pet, I grumbled... "Jocelyn, you know what I mean." "I need you to tell me Richard... I put it this way... I'm not guessing well what people want... It's all Right... But I have to know what you want... "I was physically so close to the edge that I was worried I might start crying... I breathed deeply...... And without looking at her, realizing that I would never be able to complete my thinking if I did, I said, "Jocelyn, I want us to go back to your room and make love sweetheart." I wasn't sure she was going to hit me, or just walk out quietly... But a hand on my arm was signaling her message... I look at her and she said with a shivering smile... "This may make me crazy... And maybe I'm wrong about that, but I'd enjoy that too, Richard! "Her room was awkward for a moment inside her room... Until I just shouldered her, and said... "Let's take it slow... Could we just kiss? "She was melting in my arms... Relaxed that something had to be done now, and that it was OK to just let it unfold at its own rate.

The touch was gentle and... Though gradually escalated. I don't remember what a hug it was... Lots of kisses.... Or a blurry embrace that developed and took on a life of its own. A kiss for air or pose that never ceased... A kiss like a fire that started tiny and then engulfed everything within control. I don't know when the tongue comes first... Or who the language is... Then, he got involved, but the kiss switched from the lips to a tongue dance... Playful at times... Choreographed, at times... Or sometimes, like an invading army. She caught my tongue in the roundness of her mouth at some point and she started a movement back and forth and all I could think of for the entire world was that she gave my tongue a "heart"... And in response, her tongue started to explore me and a "thrusting" movement began in my mouth, and the sexual activity was so fascinating that I found myself as hard as a rock imitating what was going on in my mouth against her breasts. Our hands were all but disconnected from the rest of our bodies... feeling hers on my back and mine on hers... From the fatness of the chest under the shoulder blades and arms, to the elegance of the small back, to the soft swell of the hips.

My hands moved between us and felt the swell of her chest. They were squeezed into my chest ... a fun mixture of hardness and softness ... but she was pressing herself on me and indeed she had the effect it had on me I'm happy that I knew. Shrugging her breasts, felt the nipple bud under her clothes with thumbs ... and she was still starving in my mouth ... I just explored my tongue Swirling, felt her mouth confirming the impact of each new note with my hand on her chest.

I moved up my hand to her buttons and began to struggle with them... and she stopped! I thought perhaps I had gone to far, but she smiled and said, "let me do those" and I watched as she removed her jacket and then slowly... knowing how sexy she was going... unbuttoned her blouse and pulling it free over her shoulders.

She came back again and the warm intoxicating feel and taste and smell of her skin were incredible... The body in her hole seemed to have almost electric socks to touch it.

I closed her, unsnapped the bra, and let her hand massage her back without distraction. Kneading the muscles of her back and feeling her relax into my arms. Her arms dropped down to her sides and her bra slipped forward and with a little wiggle landed on the floor. She reached out, placed her hands on my shoulder, and pulled us so that her nipples could be pushed into my chest.

I wanted to feel the softness of her chest. .. And her stiffness climbed on them ... against me. I took off my jacket, loosened my tie and started off the shift button.

"Let me sigh ..." she said in a wink, "I love helping men take off their clothes." She did it well ... first my shirt, then my undershirt, was pulled away from me.

Without the word of coordination, we left a little to just meet each other. "What do you think about older men?" And "What do you think about young women?" And we became nervous laughter.

"Oh, I love your firm breasts ... there are those who don't want to be wanted by those who have such vitality and life," I said. "I love the way you have treated me for the last two days... so tender and considerate... like a woman... you make me feel special... cherished" she said. "You are someone to be cherished" I said, "Someone who should have the very best... and someone who can be your equal!" "My equal... I've never wanted someone to be my equal... nor for me to be theirs. I've wanted mentors and encouragers, friends and lovers. I find in you something special that I like... and it's not equality... you treat me unique and I love that! Most guys my age are basically wanting to "use" me... to take care of them or their needs.." "Sweetie... don't become so sure that I'm above flaws... remember I want you... and that may be to "use" you." "Giving as you are getting isn't "using"... it's called loving!" "Then I want to "love" you.... I want to get and to give... to make your life pleasant for these few moments... " And we both knew the implications of that next beyond without it being said... there would be decisions made, but for the moment the only decision made without ever being spoken was that we were going to be using/loving one another with mutual consent and determination. The First Time She stepped back into my head... And I asked if she'd changed her mind.

There was an anxious expression in her eyes, and she eventually took a deep breath, putting her hands behind her, and I heard a zipper's distinct sound as she unpacked her jeans. Slowly she put her hands down between her knees, and slowly pulled down her pants with her smooth thighs. As her trousers slipped down her knees to expose the top of her underwear. Just before her trousers fell under her femininity... She kept eating, and... And he said...... they said... "Thy hand! "In an effort to be as intentionally seductive as she was out of her nervous tension, I unhooked my shirt, unsnapped my jeans and started to slide the zipper down... And then without foresight... My trousers were slipping off my knees. I missed the weight of the keys which billfold, and made it impossible for me to mimic her seduction... And to my humiliation I looked down to see my trousers with white underwear crumpled at my feet then my erection was visible! I could've heard of nothing more charming than to smile at her and say... "Oops! Oops!"She was crying... His hands cover her face to try to hide her laughing... Her breasts shake and her trousers slip to her thighs... And I just smiled! Looking at us together... It did break the ice. We were so unsure about how to be seductive and to try too hard to be sexy, and now we both just reached out and hugged together and smiled.

I took off my jeans and sat down at the bed's bottom. I took off my feet and pulled my boots off and then shifted to her... Pulling off its shoes... And her panties looked incredibly amazing. She's been washed, and naked... A stunning view. I looked at her face and her eyes glazed as she walked up the bed to make the room as she spread out her legs for me. I am curious about what I should be doing. I'd love to touch her, and feel her humidity... Or to have her feeling discovered with my tongue, but she reached out and pulled me to her face... To her eager lips and a smile that wound me around. Her thighs became a comfortable saddle and against my hardness I felt her wetness... To step toward me, to push me... to resist me. All I could do was break the kiss long enough to mouth a single word...

"And now?" She touched and led me to herself between us... So, I got caught up in... With her lips. I could hardly breathe as I felt the entrance was beginning... Just a little, just... And some more. The most precise recollection of that moment was the massive heat coming from her heart as she enveloped me. The thrusting took on primitive significance. I stared in her eyes but didn't find any words... Light moaning was audible, like pouring gasoline on a fire. I glanced around and wanted to explain that what I most wanted was to satisfy her, to please her... Yet she stared at it with her eyes fixed and I heard a sound coming from somewhere inside her mouth. When volume and tempo rose it finally registered... And it brought our hips a rhythm.... "Do it, do it, just do it... "And... And I did... We just... we did... And somewhere we were both convulsed in the hysteria of that moment... Heaving her stomach and curling her in a fetal position with me still inside her... And in that convulsing cavern I burst... Leaving me in her dark waters.

The shudders spread through us both intensely and my lips clasped firmly for a moment as the whole core of my being moved from me through her... And at that moment when my wellbeing came back, I looked in her eyes, and there was a time when her eyes were set and the light was gone... And then she was smiling... So, I knew at the heart of her being that I had hit her.

I broke down on her... Beware of dropping my weight down... Then my head rests on her pelvis. It was positively intoxicating... Sucking air through my lungs, battling the desire to move through our... And her lower abdomen's smooth, bare skin proved a cushion to my eyes. The sticky textures and the intense sex smell from her womanhood made it difficult to just relax fully.

In a second, then... The breath gushing subsided and my face fell on the smooth skin of its lower stomach, I sought the fragrance that took me back to my senses. A newly' fucked' woman's scent... And as I hugged her, I was attracted to look for her being's middle crevice. I wasn't sure how she'd pay attention to this... So freshly sat back from our lovemaking concentration... But there came a tingling and a moaning with each kiss... And her hips scotching to make the more open

When my tongue started exploring her mons, the thighs were wriggling hoping to find only the precise spot that seemed "just perfect." I discovered with careful patience that the line that led to her cleft's upper vee was the one that yielded the best results.

A lick who trimmed her cleft took away her breath... And with my tongue stretching to the limit, I found that I could reach her from the very tops of her cleft to the very back where the combination of juices so holes were more stressful to know the differences. Long slow licks revealed the flowers of her womanhood at the full length of my tongue and the flowing circular exploring of my tongue further opened her up. Her legs divided, and her feet cupped her hips to make it look like the part of a flight-ready butterfly... She appeared more and more eager for the flight with each lick and her legs began to flail as she learned the satisfaction of being content with nothing but to suffer and enjoy. I just suck it gently... And quick. For optimum touch, I flattened my tongue and stretched it as tightly into a spear to reach it as deeply as humanly possible. I flicked her clit's throbbing protrusion and let my tongue handle it as a small "punching bag" tossing it as skilfully as a fighter's two hand training for a big battle.

She shifted her hands to get all her sensitive parts in contact with my jaw and my lips... Yet I knew that when her hand reached down, we entered paradise, she took two hands full of my hair, pulling me like the reins of a horse to "rail" me to another gut-wrenching climax.

The first one with like a considerable spasm is bringing her head and knees together... Just like a giant horse in Charlie. But this one was like a seizer with lots of tiny convulsions wracking her until she laid lifeless. As my senses were coming back and my breath was moderating to fill my lungs with oxygen... I was scared of her... And still...... still... She just stopped breathing?

I shifted to her face and saw that tired look, but I was sure that either she had gone out in fatigue... Or just fell asleep... I cuddled with her, and in a naked embrace, we fell unconscious to oblivion.

The Eccentric Millionaires

The Brolins were called the Eccentric Millionaires of Westchester County. They were only a young couple for being rich. Bruce had inherited his money from his grandfather Mitchell, an investment agent. His wife Nancy was attached to the Spinks family that had mining interests all around the world.

They were very well-known for enjoying hoaxes, throwing amazing parties and generally making a nuisance of themselves. It was uncommon to start the local newspaper without seeing them and it was seldom in a fantastic light.

James Winfield knew them since they often came to the drug store where he worked. Nadine Green was familiar with the couple. She was the secretary in the veterinary clinic where they attracted their dreadful Irish hound, Dugan. Neither of those young people understood the Brolins nicely, nor did they understand one another, and were surprised when they'd been invited to a celebration at 'the huge mansion.'

The official invitation stated, should they accept, they'd be picked up by the Brolin's chauffeur. Further details contained spending the evening dancing, dining and, since it was anticipated to go on rather late, they'd be accommodated for the night. Both were somewhat reluctant since they believed they were stepping outside of the course, but finally consented to go for the experience.

James and Nadine arrived in the sprawling mansion at about 7pm and were seated together for the meal. Later on, they chased a few occasions to a live group, but by 9.30pm the artists were led home and provided a light bite. Then it was off to find their chambers. It did look quite odd to retire at this early hour, especially since the Brolin's had a reputation for maintaining their neighbors, that was a substantial distance away, awake with their loud music before sunrise.

Their rooms were adjacent to each other using a shared bathroom in between. The doorways leading into it couldn't be secured. Not just that, the doorways were created so that by the interior, they didn't seem like doorways in any way, which gave a false sense of security. Unbeknown to the couple, there were many hidden cameras watching their every move and downstairs at the library other guests had gathered to watch them on a string of monitors.

Bruce was taking bets on if the couple, who'd hadn't met before that night, could fuck each other prior to breakfast.

"That's all that contemporary childhood believes about," said Bruce, then laughed. "Sex is only a game to them if you only watch."

Comfortably seated and sipping their drinks, buddies were riveted into the displays and prepared to place their bets. Only Ashley VanCleve and her husband said they thought the couple would adhere to their beds.

Since the grandfather clock in the hallway chimed in at a quarter after ten, Nadine stripped off showing her stunning nubile figure.

"Just look at those tits," exclaimed Walter Mertion-Fitz Simmonds, getting a fast kick in the shins from his wife, Hilary. He didn't need to tip them out for each man to jack off as he leaned forward to have a good look.

Nadine, not imagining that James also had access to the toilet, entered the shower, which was totally open and started to sponge herself down. Harry Thoms, although he'd been a physician and watched nude women virtually daily, got so excited he started to fondle his wife's breasts and she didn't appear to mind one bit.

Matters got even hotter when she washed between her thighs and appeared determined to create a comprehensive job of it. Sven Lingard started to play pocket and Richard Niems was finding it very hard to breathe.

"When the fuck is the dumb kid going to go in there?" cried Walter. "Look at him, he's just sitting on the mattress dreaming."

Nadine was leaning over the washbasin cleaning her teeth when Jim decided he was ready to retire. He would also; after all, there was piss all else to do. There was no TV in the room, no magazines, books or videogames. Without any better choices before him, he figured he would have a hot shower and curl up at that very comfy looking bed. When James stripped away, it was the ladies' turn to suck their breath. The guys did so also, but theirs was a gasp of jealousy. Though his dick was in 'rest mode', it was a creature.

"Imagine having up that your twat!" cried Walter's wife, Emily. "It would provide you a lump in the throat."

The girls all laughed, but Harry's wife, Linda, was particularly impressed. She reached beneath her short skirt to finger himself. It didn't go unnoticed. A couple of the other girls decided to join in. The air in the room became highly sexually charged and there was every sign that an orgy could break out at any moment.

When James entered the toilet nude, Nadine was leaning across the basin. Her bum was jiggling from side to side in front of him. Though he tried his best to stay calm and respectful, his dick dismissed all efforts of self-control and started to rise. And when his penis rose ... it actually climbed!

"Oh, I'm sorry," he stammered, preparing to escape back into his room.

She simply turned and shrugged. "Well, we've seen each other nude now, so it is no big deal. Go right ahead and take your shower."

Nadine then glanced down and watched his vertical dick point directly at her.

"Oh my God!" she exclaimed, then smiled. "It seems you fancy me!"

"I really do," he responded, blushing a little.

"Well, I fancy you, so what exactly are you going to do about it?"

James moved ahead, slipping his arms around her waist and slamming his dick into her belly. The kiss that followed was filled with fire and tongue. Her tits rubbing against his chest made his dick grow harder and she dropped her hands down to touch his cock.

He wasn't the only one who believed in the awakening of this large horny creature. Walter and Emily were on precisely the same seat, half nude and pawing all over each other. Linda had shot her finger from her crack and had replaced it with Harry's. The Brolin's, needing to acquire a full-blown orgy penalized, was totally nude and Bruce was fucking her from behind as she leaned on the fireplace mantel.

It'd been Nadine that required the initiative and encouraged James to her bedroom. She leaped on the mattress, offering up her amazing body. He sat on the edge of the bed, leaned on her and started to suck on her erect nipples. The sexy secretary sighed as he moved his hands down and fingered her shaved pussy. In reality, because his spirited pussy massage lasted, she began to whimper like a young woman.

Everybody in the library had been so active fucking everyone else that they didn't see Nadine diving James' dick into her mouth. Nor did they see him running his tongue around the rim of her cunt. The whole home was in total chaos, with yells and groans and yells and flying limbs.

The second when James penetrated her hot wet pussy for the very first time it escaped everyone's notice except for Nadine. He really had to force his massive dick to her as if she was a virgin. She held tightly onto his forearms because he gradually worked his way in. Her sweet twat was really modest, but it seemed like she couldn't adapt the entire being. With a few grunts and groans, he was able to push it all of the ways in.

She took in a massive breath as he slowly pumped. Her ass started to squirm a bit as she desired him to grow the speed. No problem! James began to ram her with gusto, nervous to cum inside the ever-tightening love tube. This induced Nadine to create disgusting monster sounds and to yell, "Fucking hell!" followed by, "I'm cumming, I'm cumming! Shiiit!"

Even after he'd stuffed his fresh acquaintance with a huge load of his creamy goo, James didn't wish to shoot out his tremendous knob from her. Actually, he'd loved to only keep slamming off on her, to see whether he would cum again, but Nadine appeared tired. She bent down to lick the final of drops of semen bubbling from the end of his dick, but they realized that she'd had about as much pummeling because she would endure for a single night.

The following morning, the couple were grinning and holding hands under the desk while the other guests seemed finished with their fucking. Linda, who clearly hadn't showered, had traces of semen on her face and Richard was so exhausted he could barely do any basic tasks like preparing the simple breakfast of bacon and eggs. .

James and Nadine couldn't thank the Brolins enough for bringing them together.

"Oh, it is us who should thank you. I believe the simple fact that you 'arrived' made cumming a joy for everybody else," said Bruce, winking at his wife.

The Betrayer

Mary didn't want to be here.

She would rather be home sleeping her whole day away. But that would mean placing herself in direct opposition with her mother, the First Lady of a church, and her father, a very devout Christian who has been building up his reputation as a pastor for the past eight years. It wasn't like she'd asked to be born into a family so religious, but here she was, an eighteen-year-old blonde who was yet to have any of the liberties that comes with adulthood.

If she had her way, she wouldn't be here, clad in an outrageously modest skirt and a long-sleeved top, without the slightest touch of makeup on her face. She hated to go about flaunting her freckles. She wouldn't be so bothered if there were only a few of them sprayed across her nose. But no, she had much more than she considered normal. However, a touch of make-up was unacceptable because she needed to be 'Christ-like' when she went out to declare the gospel with her parents.

Being a pastor's daughter didn't have to be so hard, or did it? She had a feeling that all of this would be different and a whole lot easier to live with if they resided in one of those big cities. But here they were, in a small town filled with judgmental self-loathing people who only felt good about themselves when they made someone else feel like shit. Her skirt was a few inches past her knees. If it was a little shorter, everyone would speak ill of the pastor's daughter and her overly dramatic mom would cry, speaking of how her 'impropriety' had brought shame to their blameless family and a reproach to the Lord.

Mary knew all of that. She'd been there before, and sadly, it wasn't a situation she wanted to face ever again.

Eager to escape the scorching sun, she counted down to when she would return home. She hated the burning sensation on her feet as the sun's heat slipped through the spaces in her sandals, roasting her legs like barbecue.

Too lost in her thoughts to pay attention to the ground she walked on, she didn't realize there was a fist-sized stone in her path until she kicked it with her left foot. She jumped and yelped, but held back from cursing. In her moment of disorientation, her Bible slithered away from her grasp and landed on the hard, dusty ground.

"Oh, great!" She rolled her eyes as she bent over to pick up the book.

"You alright, Mary?" the girl beside her asked.

Mary turned sideways with a stiff smile. "Of course. Why wouldn't I be?"

"Well, I'd say you didn't wanna be here."

Mary had begun walking again, but Naomi's words had her stopping dead in her tracks.

"I'm sorry if my words were offensive," Naomi said.

"No," Mary said. "That's not it."

She thought for a moment, her eyes never leaving Naomi's. Not even for a moment had she thought that her real emotions could peek through her false front. She could have sworn the boredom she felt was anything but obvious. She'd always thought that a polite smile and a feigned display of zeal was all she needed to fool her family, the church, and even herself into thinking she was a saint. Now though, with Naomi's comment about her not wanting to be here, she wondered how much of her emotions were out in the open. And more importantly, who else could see these things besides Naomi.

A voice in her head told her there was no cause for alarm. Naomi after all was the person she was closest to. The girl was not only a member of the church but was also her cousin. So, Mary would be a damned good actress to pretend for so long around a girl who claimed to have Sherlock Holmes'' kind of mastery over the science of deduction.

"That obvious?" Mary asked after staying silent for what could have been forever.

 "Probably not." Naomi shrugged. "I guess it's because we have a lot more in common than you think."

"Are you saying…"Mary trailed off with a smile.

"Yes, May. I, just like you, do not have a heart for these things. Now that we are done with high school, hopefully, our overly religious parents will let us study in those big cities and we'll get to be who we truly are."

Naomi chucked. Mary did too.

"Probably even consider a change of name," Naomi added with a shrug.

"Probably?" Mary laughed harder, and then she frowned. "No, definitely. I do not like the name Mary."

She had never liked the name Mary, even when she was way younger. When Naomi had chosen to call her May instead, the girl had instantly become her favorite person. She should have known they had a lot more in common.

"Of all names though, they had to call you Mary." Naomi clicked her tongue, distaste evident in her eyes as she made a face.

"What am I? Some girl who got pregnant before getting to taste how damned good a cock is?"

"Hush!" Naomi turned around. "We are toast if they hear us talking about things like these."

"Yeah, right."

***

 "You expecting anyone?" Trey asked, glancing sideways at his brother Devin.

Devin shook his head, but didn't look away from the television screen in front of him.

The brothers were in the final minutes of a football match and in Trey's moment of distraction, he knew his brother would gain the upper hand. He glanced at the door. He didn't have a lot of friends, so no one ever came to visit him. He wasn't complaining or anything though. He had his PlayStation 4 to keep him company, and then there was Devin his brother.

Just like him, Devin didn't have a lot of friends, unless you counted the girls who came visiting because they couldn't get enough of his cock. He had seen his brother's cock more times than he could remember, so he knew just why the girls couldn't stop coming. Truth be told, they would always beat a path to their door. If there was anything Devin invested in, it was his body. While he worked hard to build up the rest of his body, he never left out his cock. Trey had walked in on him using penis pumps and cock enlargement creams a couple of times, so he could say that Devin's cock was way bigger than it used to be. The extra length and girth Devin's cock had earned could make Trey want to enhance his own cock as well, but at eight inches long, he didn't think there was a need for any of that.

"Think they're gone now?" Trey asked.

Devin shrugged, too engrossed in the match to say another word.

Trey set down his console and proceeded to open the door. His face paled at the sight of two women in front of him. Although he had never seen them before, he knew at once who they were. They were dressed in outrageously modest outfits, their hair stuck beneath tight scarves, but the locks of hair peeking through told him they were blonde-haired. As though their outward display of propriety wasn't enough to announce that they were 'Followers of Christ, they had their Bibles to make it all clear. And he was not one to listen to the doctrines of these people.

"Good afternoon," the first of them said.

"Not interested!" Trey moved to shut the door, but the second blonde made a frantic effort to stop him.

"You won't even see what we have to offer?" she asked.

"I already told you..." he started, and then he smiled. "Oh my, pardon my rudeness."

Was he thinking of sending them away? Beneath their extreme modesty, he saw the beauty in their eyes. The girls were young, probably younger than his twenty years of age. He glanced behind them and there was no other preacher insight. Their church was stupid to leave two young girls unguarded. It was a sight Trey didn't see too often, and he had no idea when next he would get another chance like this.

"Oh, it's okay," the first girl said. "I am Naomi and my sister—"

"May," the second said, flashing him an almost enchanting smile.

"Wanna come in?" he asked. "There is so much I wanna know."

He stepped aside and opened the door wider, letting the unsuspecting girls into his house. He grinned as Devin glanced at him with a face wrinkled with confusion. And when he winked at Devin, Devin responded with a knowing smile. They had always joked about teaching preachers a lesson, and the girls looked good enough to fuck.

Trey closed the door behind him. "By the way, I'm Trey, and this is my brother, Devin."

Devin winked at them. The girls smiled. Or were they blushing? Trey could have sworn their cheeks reddened when Devin winked at them. He had a feeling that beneath the layers of clothing was a sultriness he would love to explore.

"Please sit." He gestured at a couch.

"Thank you," the girls chorused.

They sat beside each other, and the second girl engaged him in a conversation he didn't want to be a part of. Her name was May, he remembered. He sat on the armrest of Devin's couch, and while he pretended to listen to May, Devin couldn't be bothered about any of that. He didn't take a break from his game. Well, at least he turned down the volume of the TV.

Trey knew he had to act. He didn't think the girls were allowed to spend so much time away from the other church members. He would hate the moment to pass without him getting to do what he had always dreamed of. So when the girls started to read scripture, he knew there was no better time to act.

"I should come close so I can read along," he said.

He rose from beside Devin and proceeded to sit beside May. He liked that one. She was blonde, blue-eyed and very beautiful. Even her unfashionable outfit couldn't make her any less beautiful.

"Come over here you idiot," Trey said to Devin.

Devin feigned reluctance, and then he sat beside Naomi. All four of them were slender, so they could fit into the couch. It was a tight space though. Just perfect.

"Now, Trey, I was saying..." May resumed where she left off, but Trey didn't give her a chance.

He plucked the Bible out of her hands and placed it on the stool on his side of the chair. Before May could say a word, he covered her lips with his.

She withdrew from him. "What are you doing?"

He slipped his left hand between her legs, groping her pussy through her skirt.

"Please..." she moaned.

Was she begging for him to stop or for him to fuck her already? Trey decided that she was begging him to continue. There was an undiluted lust in her eyes. From the corner of his eye, he could see Devin kissing Naomi just as hard. The girl, just like May, was also putting up feigned resistance. But she should know she didn't stand a chance against a man as robust as Devin.

Trey covered May's body with his and yanked down her skirt.

"Please, wait—" May cried, still feigning resistance.

She made an attempt to vacate the chair, but he slammed her back down and ripped off her panties. He hadn't expected the fabric to rip so easily, but it did anyway, bringing her pussy into full view. She tried to clamp her legs shut but he peeled them apart and buried his head between them. His tongue slipped right in, past her pussy lips.

"Oh, yes…s" She shamelessly moaned.

The girl was wet between her legs, her pussy lips swollen with what could have been arousal. He reached deeper with his tongue, and then he started to flick it around, mixing his spit with her pussy juice.

"Please!" she cried. "Show me the true meaning of pleasure. It doesn't matter that I'm the Pastor's daughter."

Trey paused. "Really?"

May nodded.

"I'll fuck you until you ask for more!" He glued his right index finger and his pointer together and shoved them inside her.

She cried and jumped from sheer pleasure, but he pinned her down, shoving his fingers deeper until they could go no further.

"I am a virgin, you idiot!" she snapped. "I wouldn't want to be limping when I join others!"

"Well, there's a way around that!" Trey said.

With his fingers still inside her, he yanked down his pants, bringing his huge cock out of hiding. He grabbed her left leg and hung it over the armrest of the chair so her ass was in full sight. Her tight ass didn't have the luxurious wetness of her pussy, but he could fix that with his spit.

 "Are you a virgin as well?" he heard Devin ask.

"I'm not a pastor's daughter," Naomi replied with a chuckle.

Trey glanced at her and found her parting her legs to let Devin in. She moaned as Devin slipped inside her. His cock throbbing with anticipation, Trey returned his attention to May and was stunned find her rubbing her own pussy and moaning quite loudly.

"Virgin, huh?" He raised a brow.

"I'm trying to open up my ass to let your cock you idiot!" she hissed.

For a girl so pretty, she had a flaring temper, and for a preacher's daughter, she was one hell of a bitch. Trey wasn't complaining though. He wanted to fuck her hard enough to leave her sore for talking at him in that manner. Her temper would make him do just that, without an ounce of regret for being so hard on her.

No girl had ever called him an idiot. Much less a stranger.

Fueled by a need to make her pay for bruising his ego, he decided against spitting on his cock to ease the friction when he slipped into her ass. He planted his cock at her entrance, pinning her down as he thrust right in.

There was no building up or going easy.

He thrust hard enough to tear her anal muscles as if they were made of fabric as light as her panties. Lucky her, they weren't.

May's soft moans filled his ears as he shoved his cock inside her. She squirmed, whimpering as she tried to fill her asshole with his big cock but then, Trey wanted to be the one controlling the pace, and not her. She made another loud seductive moan and Trey almost lost himself in pleasure. He grabbed her arms, pinned them to the chair and tried to shove his full length inside her. Her ass clenched hard around him and her eyes hardened, flashing with emotion he recognized as ecstasy. He knew that she was enjoying every bit of his ministrations. Her shivering body and her moans had betrayed her.

"Jesus, Trey!" she gasped. "Is this all you fucking got?"

Trey looked up into her eyes, and then he smirked. He knew her type. He knew that although she was already in the cocoon of sexual bliss, she wanted him to feel like a lesser man.

"No," he said. "But thanks for asking."

He heaved her off the couch and slammed her down on the floor. Without giving her a moment to adjust to her new posture, he flipped her over so she lay flat on her chest. He grabbed her hips and yanked them toward his body. She responded with a whimper as he forced her on all fours. She didn't even try to move away. It was as if she was faithfully waiting for his dick to claim her asshole. Without lingering any longer, he thrust into her ass and wrapped her hair around his fingers. He started to thrust in and out, tugging at her hair with each thrust.

May was moaning now, her ass clenching and unclenching. She breathed hard and fast, as though she'd been in a marathon.

Trey chuckled. "Funny how I am yet to fully enter you and you're already moaning."

He spanked her ass.

"Is it in yet?" she asked.

"What the fuck?"

"Sorry, I can't help it. You're just so tiny that I don't know if you're fully inside—"

She was trying to make him fuck her harder with her words and he knew it. The bitch sure loves a good cock.

Trey slammed hard, shoving his full length inside her with one fluid move. May swallowed the rest of her words. All Trey could hear was a soft cry of pleasure, and then there was another, a much louder cry as he started to pound.

"Oh Trey," May cried. "Please fuck me harder. Don't you—"

A knock at the door cut her off.

"Shit!" she whispered. "My father?"

"Who is it?" Devin asked voice raised.

Trey glanced back and found him balls-deep in Naomi's tight pussy, slowly thrusting.

"Just the local pastor," a man said from behind the door. "Have any preachers come this way?"

"You know," Trey whispered, tugging so hard at May's hair that her head dipped backward, toward him, "I could say yes and ask him to come in."

"Please don't." She shook her head.

"Give me a reason not to." He loosened his hold on her.

She crawled away, and then she turned around to lay on her back. She parted her legs, her hands reaching between them to part her pussy lips.

"Fuck my pussy," she said.

"Hello?" the pastor called again.

"No preachers!" Devin yelled back.

Trey crawled toward May and crept between her legs. He held her thighs apart, kissing her lips as he mounted her. She kissed him back, her lips soft and moist.

"Do you really want this?" he asked. "Do you want to lose it to me, May?"

Trey had no explanation for this, but for the first time since he got naked with May, this wasn't about teaching her a lesson. There was something different and he didn't know what it was.

"Do you?" he asked again.

She nodded.

Trey heaved his body off her and helped her to her feet. "Pick a date."

"Tonight. I'll be here."

"Promise?"

She nodded, an innocent smile creeping to her face. "Promise."

Unable to Pull Itself Out

The fact is, you will never really know anyone. In fact, the more you think you know them, the larger your blind spots become. It's convenient to think that, because you seem to know a person like the back of your hand, you can't have overlooked a big thing. Worse, once you've reached this point, you 're going to stop looking for blind spots. You 're going to be happy with the information you have. You 're getting complacent.

This tale stems from such complacency. My mom made a promise to a friend of mine, and that friend embraced it without doubt. She'd learned enough amazing stuff about me in the past, so what could be hiding in the dark corners of my mind?

In fact, a lot.

You see, I 'm pretty perverted. Okay, I admit that easily and proudly. I'm not a degenerate anymore. I treat women with the respect and dignity they deserve at all times in my daily life. It just happens that, in my nightly life, I often consider women to be "less than." Specifically, some of them become women less and sex more — pure, objective sex.

It often occurs that, on occasion, my nighttime life intrudes unexpectedly into my everyday life.

Yeah, after all, I think there's a bit of degeneracy in me. I 'd say, however, that's pretty well covered up by my other attributes. It's all about percentages, isn't it? It doesn't really matter how much you do it, just as long as it's a small percentage of everything you do, doesn't it? Eh. Yeah, that sounds good.

Now, where have we been? Ah , yes: what's lurking in the shadows? So, with a voucher, the pressure of the coming deadline, and a few alternatives, I slipped into Jen's house to take care of her pets while she was away for the weekend. If I recall right, she would have been quite unexpectedly selected by her office to introduce her new product to a business conference or something like that. At the end of the day, the reason was of no consequence.

I 'm sure you 're just wondering what my particular perversion is. Okay, that's pretty straightforward. The roots of this are not (Freud would have a field day with them), but it is, in and of itself.

I have a fascination with intimate clothing: arms, panties, slippers, corsets, cufflinks, teddies. The list is going on. My favourite in this collection, however, is the bras. There's something about them: a talent of their design, an ambition to create them, a scale that ranges from cute to sexy to stunning to elegant. There's something distinctly feminine about them, a sign of being a woman, but they can also be deeply girly. They 're made visible, and you can still catch a glimpse of them on a woman, no matter what she's wearing.

Yeah, it's so obvious that my main obsession is for the bras. There is, however, one particular downside to the bras, which takes us to the completely perverted dimension of this. It's almost impossible to masturbate with a bra, and masturbation is what the perversion is all about.

To take something that women wear under it, as a sort of last resort cover for their dignity, something that only the four walls and their lovers see, something that is the essence of anonymity, something that is so important to them—to take it away from them, into my world and under my influence, and to use it for my most basic needs, is equal to taking it away. It's even better in some ways, because they'll never learn that way. They will take these once soiled objects and wear them again, assuming that this clothing is still clean, that it will cover them, when, in reality, they are degrading themselves by draping it over their naked bodies.

There can be no way that this really is perverted.

And with that, I'm A-OK.

The trick, however, is actually to be able to defile them. I may rub my cock on a bra all day long, but I can't make the same effect as I can with something fluid and malleable, like a pair of panties. Now, the shoes, they can make a statement.

Taking soft , warm cotton or smooth, lurid silk, draping it over my cock, standing at the 5/4 mast (no erection like this), and wrapping my hand around it (firm but not tight) to slide up, up , down (slowly, at first, then faster, faster) until my body arches in one gorgeous surprise, and my cum spills up from my balls to be wrapped in that sensuous fabric — nothing like that.

A quick wash and dry, carefully put it back where they came from, and she'll never know. She'll never know that, in a week's time, she'll be walking around town, and by the way of those easy jewels, my cock rides against her cunt, and my cum mingles with her juices.

And all it takes is one complacent move to get me to creep into your universe and use you like that.

That brings us to Jen, then. I wasn't going to meet her until later (she left her house key with my mom), but I was glad to have my own version of her in the meantime. I pictured a beautiful, educated and cultured woman — a woman who would be mortified by what I was trying to do to her.

When I got out of her house after work that Friday, I felt like I had the whole world at my disposal. No more digging through loads of laundry in the laundry room, hoping to find something worth jacking with, praying that the door doesn't swing open to reveal me with two fistfuls of laundry in hand — a great way to get kicked out of college. No, for the next three days, I had a woman's full wardrobe at my disposal — my intimate choice — and I had all the time I needed to really enjoy myself.

I 'd be lying, if I were to say that I did anything other than making a beeline for her place. I just couldn't have controlled myself. In a moment, I found her dresser, and I started going through it, drawer by drawer. It only took a couple of openings before I found out what I was looking for: underwear. Row after row, each of them neatly folded and stacked. I saw them in a panic, pulling at this, that whatever caught my attention. I held a pair up to my face and breathed deeply, a sweet, fresh scent filling my ear, happily fogging my mind. My favourite pair — robin's egg blue, lace trim on the bottom, body made of silk, bound together on the sides with bands of lace — these I placed on the bed before going on.

What I was always looking forward to lying elsewhere, and it only took a few more opportunities before I find them. Yeah, Pants. Glorious weapons, guy. I felt like I was in the clouds. I took each of them out, one by one, observing them. My favorite — white cups with a black band, a lace web of black and white flowers on top of it, a delicate pink bow between the cups — I held up and nestled my face in. I imagined her boobs snuggled into it, her hard, horny nipples pressed into it, and I imagined that I would reach out and grab her, feel her soft, foldable flesh under my fingers.

My ears were ringing, my enthusiasm was so strong. I was thinking of teasing myself with these gifts, of building up and up before I eventually indulged, but I knew there was no way I could last. With my bra in one side and my panties in the other, I jumped up on my bed and began to settle in when a thought came to my mind. Why don't you get naked? Why not, in fact. Wouldn't it be more of a fantasy than to caress her bra and defile her panties, if I also invaded the place where she slept? What could be the harm, besides?

So, I stripped and laid myself down quickly. I had the feeling that I was floating, I was swimming in too many endorphins. And when I put my find on top of my cock, the silk that fell to caress my head and cover my shaft, it was like I was on a rocket, flying off to the moon. I covered my face in the bra, revealing in the way that the big cups used to consume me, and I worked my hand in long , slow strokes, savouring the soft swish of the fabric on my skin.

I was so lost in my joy that I did not hear the car pull up, the key in the lock, the door opening, the steps coming down the hall, the sound of my delight in the house. My trance has not been broken until —

"What the hell are you doing here?"

When I opened my eyes and looked up, I discovered with terror that Jen was standing in the doorway.

"What, what, what, what's going on here?"

"I ... I, uh ... It's ..." Retrospectively, I 'm surprised that I was actually able to make sentences. Terror and frustration had reduced my brain to a buzz of statics.

"You ... You 're ... That's my —! That's my —!" Jen was clearly in a similar state of shock. "And you are, you pervert!"

"Look. I — I'm sorry!" Ah, words started to come. "I'm just going — I'm going to get up and go, and you don't have to pay me or anything, just please don't tell anyone."

"Go? Go? Oh no. No, no, no. You 're not going anywhere." Her panic had become a sort of crazy euphoria. "You 're going to sit right there, and you're going to finish what you started."

"Wait. What? I can't ... I can't do that now!" Sense was flooding back, and I realised that I was still lying there, cock in hand, wrapped in her panties. I flung them to the side and shuffled back to sit at the head of the bed. I momentarily thought of covering my nakedness with her bra before I remembered how terrible that would be, and I threw it to the side as well.

"No. No. If that's what you're going to do, you 're going to do it, and you're going to do it with me, pissed off, watching you, you little snake!" she picked up her panties from the floor and threw them at me. Comically, they fell on my nose, and I slapped myself in an effort to brush them off.

"Why? Why would you like that?"

"Because I bet you came here thinking you were powerful. You thought you were sly and smart, confident I'd never find out. You thought you were going to snoop around and figure out just what you wanted, what was 'good.' You thought you could take it for yourself, and you would know my intimacy. You thought that by breaching it, you would be breaching me—"

"Please, please don't make me do this," I said. But even as I said, I wrapped my silk delight around my cock — a cock that was growing again quickly — and I resumed my play.

"And because you were so sly and smart, I would never have known it. When I put them on my body, snuggled them up against my most sensitive areas, shielded me from the world, when the cloth that brushed against your flesh brushed against mine, it would have been like your face nestled against my tits, and your cock kissed my clit. You imagined that, even if you had washed them perfectly.

"But that ..."

"But I'm in breach of you now."

Fear still ruled my mind, but the desire was creeping in. As I sat there, slowly stroking myself, working my cock up harder and harder, I couldn't help but look at the woman standing in front of me.

I learned from my mom that Jen was in her mid-twenties, and she was definitely looking at it. She looked at it in the way that makes teens swoon and college students try their hardest to get their professors out for a night in town—"Come on, Prof, come celebrate the end of the finals with me and the gang.

Her straw-blonde hair was twisted into a tight braid that fell in front of her, resting against her side. Tied around her neck was the stallion of her outfit, the lustrous fabric of which was molded to her body. Her curves could make an hourglass jealous, and her bust would lift the wrath of her peers: bountiful, high, and pert like a twenty-year-old.

My gaze went back to her face, my eyes closed with hers. I could practically hear the crackling of the fire that burned inside them and the steady grinding of her teeth as they rubbed against each other. But as I continued to work myself, pulling her panties up and down over my sensitive skin, the light inside her eyes slowly faded from frustration to curiosity, and a spark of anticipation shone in them.

"Have you ever seen an older woman before? And I don't mean those cheap, fake bitches in trashy porns. I mean, a real woman — a real woman with real boobs and real lips — a woman you might reach out and touch."

"I ... I ... I ... I don't, I don't."

"Well, here you go," she said, simply, before reaching her hands behind her head and, with two little tugs on her knot, stripped down for me, her dress crashing down to the pool around her legs.

Her skin was like alabaster, no mole, no blemish, no scar, no freckle. Her nipples stood proudly on her breasts — large and hard — surrounded by the pink bubble gum pools of her areolae. And, without panties, her smooth, hairless mound spoke to a woman who carefully preserved her portrait, even if only for herself.

"Mm ... I'm great, isn't I?" she asked, looking not for pleasure, but to taunt me.

Unsurprisingly, it was working. Blood soon fled my brain, leaving rationality behind in favor of instinct — and there was really only one instinct to pursue.

For a few minutes she watched me play with myself, the sensations were growing, my anticipation was constantly rising, but my orgasm was eternally out of control, held at bay by residual fear and shame.

Eventually, putting on a pouting face and saying, "Oh, that's no fun," Jen climbed to the bed and crawled over to me. Without a comment, she threw away my hand and wrapped hers around my cock.

The woman who had just caught me masturbating with her panties was now jerking me off with them.

This is what people talk about when they say, "Crazier things have happened ..."

"This is a lot more fun for you and me," she said. "So, Billy Boy, I 'm sure you've gotten a blowjob before — maybe from that girl across the quad who isn't ready to give up her virtue but doesn't want to lose a hunk like you — maybe from that wild girl you met at a music festival — maybe you even joined the Mile High Club. But you've never been worked like this."

And she was right about that. This wasn't a simple up-and - down matter, it wasn't a fast asshole. Short and fast has given way to a long and slow process. Straight strokes have become spinning pulls. An intense, strong grip has become a soft embrace. Her movements followed a graceful, fluid, diverse melody.

And all the same, the shoes. Oh! Oh! Oh! The shoes! My cock was moulded by the sultry cloth, and every slip of it against my skin lured my orgasm closer to the surface.

Jen began pounding my cock faster and faster; my breathing became erratic; my attention became narrowed down to Jen, my dick, and her panties. Once my orgasm came in, it came in without warning. I was climbing up to it at one point, and I was climbing up to the next. My hips shook uncontrollably, almost yanking me out of Jen 's grip; my eyes clamped shut; I let go of a raw, intestinal scream.

And I emptied my semen, burst it, burst it.

When my breathing calmed and my heart came to rest, I saw that the panties were completely soaked, and Jen 's hand was sticky and muddy. Slowly, she pulled them out of my still-sensible cock to expose how the fabric had darkened from a nice robin's egg to a rich blue, flecked with the white of my cum — a reflection of her transformation from innocent to lewd.

Holding them close to her ear, she said, "Is that what you wanted? Is that a violation you've dreamed of?" Then, feigning confusion, "It wasn't a second part, was it?"

"Y-yes," I said.

"And what was that?"

"You 'd wear it. I 'd put it in your wardrobe, and one day — someday — you'd come and snatch it and wear it, and you'd be hideous, thinking you 'd be clean."

"But what if I want to be ugly? What if little boys with a mommy complex are what makes my engine really pure?" And, as she pulled out the final syllable, she pulled back to her knees in front of me, her back upright and her knees on the shoulder-width. "And, you know, I love semen. I love the way it feels against my skin." She scooped a sample in her other hand and pressed it against her breast, rolling her nipple between her fingertips. "I love the way it tastes." She gradually raised her hand to her mouth, and her tongue darted out enthusiastically to lick a tiny morsel. "And I love the sticky, sweet mixture of my pussy juice," she said. "And with that, she lowered her hand to her crotch and rubbed herself with my essence.

"And it would be such a waste, my dear little perv, to throw these panties in the washing machine, soaked as they are in your delicious cum. And what's better for you: my once-sullied, now-clean panties riding against my skin or my now-soaked, now-soiled, now-conquered lingerie coating my pussy, my sex, my flower, with your masculine offering?"

"Are you asking that?"

"I don't know anything, you are."

"I want you to rub your cum-rag panties all over your perv-loving snack."

"Oh, simple boy, I 'm going to do so much more than that." And with the determination that betrayed her lust, she swept her panty-wrapped hand between her legs and began to show the most sensuous display I've ever — and ever would — seen. Long strokes up and down her slit turned into little circles around her clit. Faster and faster, she rubbed in her rounds until she pushed three fingers inside herself, pulling her panties along with them.

There was a glimpse of pink and blue and cream between her thighs, her love and my desire and my proposal. Her body shook with every jackass of her back. I thought of myself as a twisted and disgusting specimen, but she was doubly so, revealing in my perversion. This was, literally, the woman of my dreams.

In my enthusiasm, in the lurid, the foundation presentation, in the cacophony of primary delight, I lost myself. This woman was an alcoholic, and I was a party person: wasted. My heart beat like the bass drum of Metallica, and my breaths were breathless. My once firm, then soft, then hard, then soft cock had once again become a stone. On top of that, I put her stolen bra, which had previously been thrown out of my bed. One hand rubbed a cup over my cock 's head, and the other massaged my thighs. Soon, I added my moans to hers, and the room was filled with sex.

The echo of my enjoyment diverted Jen 's attention, and her eyes shot open, staring straight into mine. Her hand paused in her ministrations, as she said, "So, some of the boy's virility has returned. Tell me, is that what you really want: to squander your dwindling reserves on a bra, just as it might be? Or would you rather ply your craft with something much more ... delicious?"

Without waiting for my answer, she took the bra out of my hand and threw it over her shoulder. She bent forward in a practiced motion and crawled toward me. Her eyes burned with lust bordering on the savage — the blazing spots of lascivious cycloids. She reached the end of her journey above me — her hands on the sides of my thighs, spread far apart. Her breasts hang like carnal church bells from her neck, swaying seductively over my ear. The trailing end of her panties dangled from the inside of her, tickling the tip of my cock.

"Tell me, young man, do you want it? Do you need it?"

"Yes , yes, yes."

"You 're hungry?"

"Yes , yes, please!"

"Here you are, sweetheart. Be happy, make me happy."

Plop. Plop.

Her knees were bent, her chest lowered, and her breast fell into my waiting mouth. I was excited to see her. My body was longing for her. My lips were fixed on her, sucking her deep inside me. My tongue was ready to meet her nipple, and I was met with a surprise on my first lick: the taste of both her body and mine. This was the nipple that spread my cum like a lotion, the nipple that held the ineffable taste of my virility.

The emotions elicited were confusion, delight, and awe. Confusion of trying myself on someone else. Delight for the flesh that is entwined with mine. And fear for the wealthy, greedy, shocking woman who kept the fate of my pleasure in her sticky palms.

Her breasts were like toys in my mouth and my hands. I massaged her mounds by cutting my hands around them, rubbing against them — running my fingertips over them, sliding on the skin, digging my nails into them, kneading her delicate flesh. My head rolled up and down, planting kisses over every inch of them. I rubbed my tongue around the base of one and up between the two. My lips were stuck in a breast, sucking it to the end of my tongue, flicking up and down and around.

My eyes were squeezed shut, invaded as I was by my job, but they were called to open an especially loud squeal — Ah! — when I clamped my teeth against her. Her face popped up above mine, a wicked smile spread over her lips, and her shimmering eyes gazed right down into mine.

"Mm, are you having a nice time down there?" she asked. "Because I'm having a helluva time up here. It's been too long since my boobs paid so much attention to them, but enough with the appetisers. Let 's move on to the main course."

She shifted her weight to one hand and put the other on my chest. She angled her fingertips to her tips and rubbed her nails in my neck. She clawed a long line down my body, but then, just before she hit my dick, she took a sharp turn on my thigh. The end of her line left her hand between her legs, and she raised her hand from me to herself.

She put her palm on her mound and placed her fingers above her sex. Even the quick, distracted touch forced the air out of her lungs. Her entire body shuddered with excitement as she slowly curved her middle finger inward, slipping it up from the bottom of her pussy to the top of her pussy, and for a moment she turned into a gasping, sucking mess as she pushed her fingertip into her clit. She almost collapsed when she plunged three fingers into herself—"Oh, god, I'm wet!"—and her fingers glistened dazzlingly as she withdrew them.

I figured she wanted to taste herself again, or maybe she wanted me to taste her. I was astonished, then, when she dropped her hand from between her legs to the middle of mine, and her fingers formed a firm grip on my cock. I was convinced that I was coming as she pulled her hand up in a slow, twisting motion. Before my mind could make the words to express my joy, I felt her tilting me back to her, then I felt a slight, warm pressure on my head.

The time had come to fulfill a dream that I never knew I had.

"Are you ready, boy?"

"This is Pope Catholi — Oh!"

It was like jumping off the bridge. I knew I was gonna make a leap from outside to inside, but there was nothing for a moment. Like air rushing past me, I felt my journey through her in vague terms — sensations that existed at the edge of awareness. But when I cut the path full through her, when her body's passion had swallowed all my body's pride, I burst through the surface of my desire in an eruption of raw emotion, wild anticipation, and unrelenting ecstasy.

"Oh — your — oh — your cunt!"

"Mm ... It's great, isn't it? It's hot and wet, and it's squeezing you like a mitten in the snow: close and soothing." She started grinding against me in slow, small circles, pushing me inside of her in exhilarating increments. My hips pushed up, hungry at her, and hers pressed down, pushing me to get as far as I could. Then, like a third hand, she started flexing the muscles inside her, gripping my cock in rhythmic pulses, teasing my erection to its limits — anymore, and I would burst. "But removing the gloves will never feel like that," she said, before she took off from me and quickly sat back down.

Suddenly, she was fucking me, pressing hard on me. The world has really turned into a blur of sights and sounds and sensations: my wild, hyperventilating breaths — her hair, falling on my face and spinning over my skin — the slap of her body hitting mine and the gentle squish of my cock plowing in and out of her — her ooh's and ah's and mm's rising in intensity and passion. My head was spinning, my whole body was tight, my cock was on fire.

"Can you feel it? Can you feel my pants?" and I could. Instead of balling up inside her, they lay down to the side so that half of my cock slipped against slick sex and half slid against smooth silk. It was a perverted playmate on one side and a perverted fascination on the other.

"Slap me," she said, in the middle of the labored breaths.

"What is it?"

"Just do it! Slap my boobs"—whack—"harder"—whack! "Harder!"—WHACK— "Harder!"—WHACK!!!

"Ah, yeah! Yeah, I can feel it now, I can feel it coming," she moaned. "And I can feel you. I can feel your body shaking with every move. I can feel the shiver flowing through your ass, up your dick, vibrating my pussy.

"I'm so close to you. Are you really close? Just a minute. You 're close, of course! I can see that in your eye — oh! Oh! Oh! Oh! Then! Then! Come with me now, you son of a bitch! "

Upon her orders, I came. I came as though it was an invasion, and I had to repopulate the universe all in one go. For an amazing, delirious moment, I lost my connection to the world around me. All I knew was my cock — possessed by an orgasm so powerful that it burned — quickly unloading gallons of cum — cradled by a pussy convulsed in an epileptic, psychotic fit — nestled against a pair of panties that would never be clean again, no matter how many times she washed them.

As I returned to the realm of the physical, my mind still spinning, and my breathing still urgent, I was met with Jen's sight upright, kneeling, her knees still spread apart, straddling me, her tits bigger, her cheeks flushed, her face set in an angel's afterglow of pleasure.

And there was a dark blue slip of fabric between her legs that began all this and the white dribble-dribble-drip that marked her end.

"So, sweetheart, I think you've offended me twice."

A Birthday Parties

Amber's birthday parties had now become a social event, and after celebrating passing the bar exam together, Jasmine and I had been invited to yet another evening at her home. For the occasion, I bought myself a nice long dress, it was perhaps a little too bold, as, in addition to a deep slit along the right thigh, the dress left both the décolletage and the back in plain sight.

"But you're going to cause a car crash with that dress, "So Jasmine exclaimed when she saw me.

"Look, more than a crash a five-car pile-up," I retorted with a chuckle. "It's just that I'm not used to such clothes."

Actually, I felt a certain discomfort when I had to wear evening dresses, ending up moving almost to a bland look or something way too dramatic, I could never find a healthy medium. In order not to arrive with one of our cars, which certainly would have ended up ticketed, we decided to take a luxe Uber, and I believe that the driver spent more time looking at us from inside the mirror than on the road.

When we arrived at the party, which for the occasion had been organized in a large mansion near Westchester, and at the entrance Amber greeted us in a too formal way.

"I would like to jump on you and do untold things to you," she whispered in my ear, "but for the moment my parents are here and I have to be a good girl."

I lost sight of Jasmine almost immediately, so I started walking around the garden, taking occasional snacks that I accompanied with champagne. I soon noticed that there was a beautiful woman staring at me, and not knowing what to do, I went to an uncrowded area of the garden even to see if she followed me. Without realizing it, she walked past me and then stopped just as she was passing me.

What struck me was that she was dressed as a man, in a black tuxedo with a shirt and bow tie. Out of the corner of my eye, I saw that a man was approaching, and a moment later I found his lips on mine.

"Tilly was looking for you," the man said timidly.

"Go away, don't you see that I'm in company." The woman replied without concealing her contempt.

The man shrugged his shoulders and then turned and disappeared among the plants.

"I'm sorry but I can't stand it, I just hope you understand it now."

"Excuses accepted, anyway I'm Paige," I said giving her my hand

"Tilly," she replied shaking my hand with a sensual strength.

We began to walk talking about trivial things; however, because it was clear that we both felt a certain attraction towards each other, and in the end, I could no longer resist.

"I must say that your lips taste good," I said, touching mine to hers.

"Yours are not bad at all," she replied taking me by the hand "Come let us look for a place to ruin your make-up."

We entered the mansion to climb two floors of stairs and found a free bathroom, where we entered at a run to then lock ourselves in. As soon as I rested my buttocks against a long piece of furniture, she was immediately upon me, giving me a long kiss in the mouth while her hand sought my thigh. I completely abandoned myself to her who did not stop a moment from kissing me first on my neck, then on my mouth, then in my cleavage. One of her hands tried with more and more intensity to get to my vagina, which was moist with passion.

"My God, you are definitely a man!" I joked, surprised by her impetuosity.

"You're the one who drives me crazy," she replied discovering my legs and then taking off my thong.

I spread my legs just enough to allow her to penetrate me with two fingers. All the while, stifling my groans with her lips.

"Lick my pussy, I want to enjoy this moment," I almost ordered her putting a hand in her hair and then pushing her head between my legs.

She made me sit on the piece of furniture and then knelt in front of me, and start a slow job made of small penetrations with her fingers, and long passages of tongue between the small lips. I wished I could scream in pleasure, but I stopped myself as I was terrified that someone would hear me. It didn't stop me completely me so she bit my lips, while Tilly was actually finger banging me with three fingers and at an intense speed. I could barely recognize the difference between them and a penis.

"Turn around, I want you all for me," she said, bringing those fingers so full of my pleasure to my mouth, that I licked greedily before turning and lifting my leg, resting it on the cabinet.

For a few moments, it felt as if Tilly had three hands, as she was able to massage my pussy, lick the little hole and at the same time slap my ass. I barely managed to open the button that held the dress on me, which once free, fell to the ground, leaving me completely naked.

"I bet you're a slut who likes it in the ass," she whispered in my ear as she ran her fingers through the groove of my ass.

"I would give you everything," I replied looking for her lips, which I found ready to accept mine.

Tilly sodomized me with two fingers, gently squeezing my breast with the other hand, and wanting to reach the peak of pleasure as soon as possible, I had no choice but to slip two fingers into my dripping wetness.

"I won't let you come so fast," she told me, making me turn again and moving a few feet away from me.

"And how you intend to do that," I asked, sitting on the cabinet to be able to masturbate more comfortably.

She began to undress by first taking off her jacket, then opening her blouse, thus showing me her breasts, a beautiful pair that did not need any support to remain in place.

"You like my tits," she asked me after another long kiss.

"Yes, they are really worth licking," I replied starting to lick her nipples.

So, we started kissing in the mouth and on the breast, almost wanting to catch our breaths, letting those little pleasures take us back to wanting to discover new ways to orgasm. But when I reached out to take her pants off, she took a step back, as if to stop me from undressing her.

"Paige, I'm not a woman."

At first, I didn't understand her words, but when she opened her pants and got a good cock erection, I was momentarily surprised, but was taken by lust and didn't care.

"I do not care anything about who you are." I said, turning around and then bend over on the little couch and she opened my pussy with her fingers, "Now grab your dick and fuck me, girl, because I just want to enjoy it."

Tilly was eager for this moment and did not lose a second. Nearly penetrating me completely with the first lunge. She alternated between moments of pure passion and intensity. She was one of the best lovers I had had in a while.

Not wanting to come quickly, I let her out of me, to be able to sit on the piece of furniture and get have her inside me in missionary position. As she was inside me, I clasped her ass, as if I was afraid that she would run away. Tilly began to kiss me with an almost animalistic lust, when she didn't touch the little button making me hold back, with much difficulty, screams of pleasure. I had a sweet and violent orgasm at the same time as her, and she stopped inside me to allow me to savor the moment.

"I wonder what this transgirl's dick tastes like," I thought to myself, so I slipped between her legs to take it in my mouth.

Tilly's penis was larger than some of the others I had taken, but it had a different effect on her, a mixture of perversion and diversity that excited me beyond measure. I started licking the tip and then running my tongue over the whole shaft, before taking it all in my mouth, holding one hand under her balls.

"But you're really a good slut," she told me putting her hands in my hair to make me stand up.

"A slut in need of your cock," I replied sitting on the bathroom cabinet again.

She placed the tip against my moist flower, then pressed her lips against mine before pushing all the rod inside, making me nearly jump with pleasure. Tilly was a violent stallion in her mount, though she never hurt me. I enjoyed without any restraint, urging her to be even more rough with me.

"Fuck me and then fuck me again." I told her, placing a hand on my pussy "Or do you prefer my ass."

"Why are you telling me? Do you want to see what it is like to get your ass taken by a transgirl?"

"Yes, and you don't know how curious I am."

"At your service," she replied smiling, before kneeling.

With an almost exasperating slowness, she made me feel the tip of her tongue go down from the crack to the anus and then turn around and immediately go up and down again. When she stopped on the little hole, she almost sucked it into her mouth, at the same time managing to stick her tongue into it. I tried to stretch out my hand on my mount of pleasure, but she slapped my hand making me understand that she wanted to be the only source of my pleasure. All I could do was enjoy her tongue and her finger, which had become a fixed presence inside me.

"Tilly, I beg you; I can't stand it any longer," I pleaded without feeling any shame for my lust.

She didn't answer me, but got up and sodomized me slowly, making me feel every single inch of her cock sliding inside me.

"I like it a little rough, keep it up, please."

As before she said nothing, and after taking a good pace, she slipped two fingers into my now soaked vagina.

"Enjoy my baby" I heard her say almost softly, just before having an orgasm.

This time, however, I didn't wait too long because I wanted to see her enjoy, so I leaned her against the piece of furniture and crouched between her legs, which she opened as much as possible as if to invite me to take her ass.

"Now I want to drink your pleasure," I said taking her penis in my hand and letting a finger slip between her buttocks.

It took me very little, in addition to sticking two fingers in her ass, to make her come and find my mouth full of her orgasm. Pleasure that I then brought to his mouth in the last long kiss before getting dressed to get out. Outside the door, we found two boys' intent on touching each other over their trousers, happy to slip into the bathroom to give vent to their desires.

We found ourselves in the party that was now fading, acting as if nothing had happened, exchanging telephone numbers with the promise to meet again as soon as possible.

"But where were you? I've been looking for you all night," Jasmine scolded me, seeing me sitting alone at a table.

"Maybe I'll tell you tomorrow," I replied as I stood up. "From the way you drop your dress I don't think you've always kept me in the loop either, my friend?"

"Ugh, you can never hide anything! Maybe tomorrow I'll tell you something, but now let's go home."

I laughed thinking about how she would react to my story with Tilly, remaining alone with the doubt whether she had had fun with one man or if it was in an orgy.

A MILF's First Lesbian Sex

Laura reinvents her life when she ends up divorced and her only child heads off to college. She wanted to experience new things and to get out of the house, so she signed up for a book club and a cooking class. Little does she know that the cooking class will turn up the heat and reinvent more than she ever thought possible.

I just never saw it coming. I really didn't. I mean, I was almost forty and divorced, with my only daughter off to college. I had a pretty good job and with her out of the house, I had reduced expenses significantly. Well, except for the college tuition of course. I was lucky; she was a smart girl and had gotten a pretty generous scholarship, so I did not have to pay exorbitant rates. Her father was chipping in a little, but I did not count on that for the basics. Usually, whatever he would send me, I just stuck into an account for her for after college graduation.

My life was smooth and quiet for the most part. Shortly after she graduated high school, I had sold off our small house for an even smaller two bedroom apartment. I used the master bedroom, of course, and the second room was a combination bedroom and study. She was a little surprised when I moved, but I think she understood. Living by myself now, I really did not want the maintenance of a full-size house.

It was fabulous being able to clean the whole place in under an hour, and having so much time back in my weekends with no yard work either. To make sure I got out of the house, I signed up for a book club and a cooking class. It seemed that I had a whole new world waiting for me. I guess I never expected just how new that world would turn out to be.

With just me to focus on, I was eating healthier and making a lot more food at home. I had always enjoyed cooking and felt bad that I did not make more homemade meals for Chelsea, my daughter. She had been so patient and understanding when the divorce went through, much more so than a normal 14-year-old should have to be. I had always worked outside of the home, so that was not a huge change.

But when I started picking up extra work at the office for the overtime pay, things started to slip through the cracks. One of which was home-cooked dinners. I still made some things. After all, if I made spaghetti on Sunday evening, we could eat on that for at least a few days.

Now that I was on my own, I was doing that quite a bit. I would make big batches of grilled chicken or soup, and then portion out my lunches and dinners for the week, including a lot of salads. It was all of the convenience of an easy frozen dinner but homemade!

The cooking class I signed up for was about cooking for one. It sounded so pitiful, but I think it was supposed to be a singles group slash cooking class. I was not interested in the 'single' part, I had not even thought of dating since the divorce.

Well, I had thought of it once. A guy from the office asked me to dinner shortly after the divorce was finalized, and I accepted. Chelsea reacted strangely, so I dropped the entire concept. Besides, I had enough to worry about without taking on a relationship too. Looking back, it was probably too soon for her. And for me, if I want, to be honest. I guess I just wanted company or something.

My marriage had been going downhill long before we filed any paperwork. It had been years since we had had sex, and to tell the truth, I was okay with that. We had gotten married young and had our family right away. I never had those crazy stories about "when I was in my twenties". My twenties included teething and potty training.

A couple of new friends from the book club told me that now was my time. That since I missed out on all the fun in my twenties, I had to live it up now. I looked at them like they were insane. I was way too old for that crazy stuff.

Instead, to burn off some extra calories, I also joined a gym near the apartment. I was not hard-core or anything, just a little time on the treadmill or in the pool. I tried one spinning class and nearly died. I was better off just doing regular things, and so was everyone around me.

One Saturday afternoon, I had finished working out and grabbed a quick shower before heading to my cooking class. I was excited about that day's menu. It was some kind of grilled chicken that you could supposedly freeze for later, or use in like a hundred different ways. It sounded perfect for me!

I noticed a new face in the room when I arrived but really did not pay any attention. I stashed my purse under my work table and started looking through the ingredients and the directions.

"Have you done this before?" the voice was quiet but self-assured.

I nodded without looking up.

"Want to be partners then?"

I finally looked in the direction of the voice and found the new face smiling back at me.

"Oh, hi there. I'm Laura," I offered my hand.

The slight young woman grinned back at me, the diamond in her nose glinting under the lights. She had long blonde hair and dark green eyes.

"Athena," she replied, "Is that a yes then?"

"Sure," I agreed a little too easily.

She seemed pleasant enough. I was a little surprised when she bent over her bag, and I spotted a large swirling black tattoo in the small of her back, barely peeking over the waistband of her tight leggings. Not to mention that while her hair was long, the underside was buzzed down almost to her scalp. Still, in the bent over position, she turned and looked up at me. I flushed pink and looked away, embarrassed to have been caught staring at her. Just then the instructor entered the room to begin class, and I was saved by the bell, so to speak.

****

We started with some kind of appetizer, diced olives and tomatoes on toasted bread. Athena smiled at me and slid the dish of olives over to my side of the table.

"If you'll do the olives, I'll do the tomatoes," her green eyes flashed when she smiled at me.

"S-Sure," I stuttered, reaching for the dish.

I had no idea why this young woman was making me nervous, but she was. I felt flush, but it could have just been from the fact she caught me staring at her tattoo.

We diced everything and dumped it into the larger mixing bowl.

"What's next?" I studied my instruction sheet.

"It looks like garlic and olive oil. Do you want to crush or pour?"

My head whipped up towards her; there seemed to be innuendo in her statement, but I could not figure out where.

"I'll pour," I offered.

"Good, I like crushing," she winked.

She actually winked at me! What the heck was going on? My poor little brain was racing in confusion.

Athena laid out several cloves of garlic and smacked them with the broad side of a large knife. She carefully peeled off the papery skin and then went to town with the sharp edge of the knife until the garlic was more like a paste. With a smooth brush, she scooped the paste onto the knife and then scraped it into the bowl.

I poured the olive oil into the mixture and was nervous because I became intensely aware that she was watching me not the bowl.

When everything was added, she grinned at me and rolled up the sleeves of her long chambray shirt. With a gleam in her eye, she stuck both hands into the large bowl and started mixing everything together with her fingers. The juicy ripe tomatoes slid around, and the olive oil made her skin glisten.

I laughed while she did it, "I don't see that part in the instructions."

"Sometimes you have to think outside the box. And just get your hands dirty."

Again with the unidentifiable innuendo.

After we toasted the little bread slices and devoured our creation, we moved on to the chicken. It was not nearly as exciting as the tapenade, but she was fun company. Her laugh tinkled like a silver bell, and she seemed very intent on making a veiled point with her continued innuendo, but I just was not catching on to the implications.

After we finished the chicken and deemed It delicious, it was time for dessert. With a practiced hand, she easily whipped up the chocolate soufflé, and we took a small break while it set. When it was ready, she held her dish up and grinned at me.

While staring directly into my eyes, she slowly slid one finger into the creamy chocolate concoction and deliberately licked it off her fingertip.

I just blinked at her. I mean, I was not good at picking up on signals, but even I could tell that one.

"Um, Athena?" I wanted to nip it in the bud and tell her that I was not 'that type.'

"Yes?" her face looked eager and hopeful with just a hint of wickedness.

"I'm not sure…" my voice trailed off. I was not sure how to phrase it delicately to this nice young woman in her tight leggings and long baggy shirt.

"Would you like to get a drink? After all, we've just had dinner together…"

I nodded, since I was clearly unable to process the words I needed.

Once we finished the food we had prepared and cleaned up our dirty dishes, we walked out together into the crisp night air.

"What a beautiful night," she breathed, her pale skin shining in the lamplight.

She pointed to our left, and we started walking. I was clutching tightly to my purse, more out of nerves than anything. After several blocks of walking, Athena stopped in front of a small apartment building.

"This doesn't look like…"

She laughed, "Like a bar? It's not, I live here. It's the closest place to get a good glass of wine. I have great taste, you know."

She ushered me inside, and I perched on the edge of the couch with my purse balanced on my knees. She giggled when she returned from the kitchen.

"Just relax, I don't bite. Well, I've been known to, but you have to ask," she gave me another wink that made me blush.

Her fingers brushed against mine when she handed me a wine glass, and I must have shivered. She sat down very close to me and put her hand on my shoulder.

"Laura, you seem rather nervous."

"Yeah, a little."

"Why do I make you nervous?"

"I guess… Because this suddenly feels like a date and I don't know what to do with that…" I admitted my fear.

"Do with what? We're just having a glass of wine and getting to know each other."

Her fingers brushed against my cheek as she tucked a stray curl behind my ear.

"Athena…"

"Just drink your wine, we're just getting to know each other," she repeated.

I had never had another woman touch me in that way. But it felt nice; I was nervous because this was all new territory but it did not put me off, and that was even scarier. With a gulp, I swallowed down the last of my wine and eased back against the couch cushions.

She slowly unbuttoned and removed her baggy shirt to reveal a very cute trim little figure, much more noticeable in just the tight leggings and snug tee shirt. Then she reclined back next to me, nuzzling into my neck and slowly slid her fingertips up my thigh. I shivered but had no desire to move away from her touch.

"You're very pretty, Laura. I noticed you in class immediately," she whispered, her warm breath tickling my ear.

"I-I noticed you too," I confessed.

"I know," she giggled, "I caught you staring at my ass."

"I was not! I was looking at your tattoo!"

"Which is right above my ass, missy."

She had me there.

The tip of Athena's tongue tickled the outer shell of my ear, and I shivered. Her breath was warm on my skin, and I seemed partially frozen in place. On one hand I liked how it felt and did not want her to stop; but on the other hand, I had no idea what I was doing and was terrified of doing something wrong.

"Just relax and let me show you," she whispered, already realizing what I was thinking.

I did not even realize I had been holding my breath until it escaped with a soft whoosh.

Her lips were soft against my neck, and I never minded the stubble in a man's kiss until I had experienced the softness of a woman's face against my skin. Her cheek was smooth as it grazed mine, and she seemed to know all the places that made me shiver. My ears, my neck, my throat.

Her slender body weighed almost nothing when she crawled up to straddle my lap. With a giggle, she slowly took my hands out from under my own thighs and placed them on her waist.

"It's okay, you can touch too," she nodded.

I rested my hands lightly on top of her hip bones, feeling her move gracefully as she bent towards me. She pressed her lips to mine gently at first, just the barest of butterfly kisses. I guess it woke something up because I found myself kissing her back and my hands started moving along her back.

Her fingers tickled the nape of my neck, and I think I let out a soft moan. It had been so long since anyone touched me like that, it was almost overwhelming. When I started kissing her back, her lips felt more urgent. Her tongue swiped across my lower lip, and when I gasped, she darted just the tip between my parted lips.

I pressed my hands against her back, trying to pull her closer. Her hips were gyrating slowly as her tongue entwined with mine. When one of my hands slid up to her neck, I felt the bristly velvet of the shaved part and rubbed it softly.

She giggled, "You like that?"

I nodded, "It feels so soft."

With gentle but firm hands, she pressed my thighs apart and knelt on the floor between my legs. In that position, her face was about parallel with my tits.

"Oh I have got to see these," she breathed with a hungry smile.

I laughed and slowly began to unbutton my shirt.

She snatched my fingers away with a pout, "But I want to do that."

I laughed and dropped my hands to the couch. As she finished the job, she left a trail of wet kisses on each inch of skin as it appeared. She licked and kissed and nibbled at my collarbone, at the upper swell of my breasts, and all the way down my tummy. By the time my shirt was completely open, I could hardly breathe. I just shivered and squirmed underneath her.

She slowly pushed my shirt off my shoulders and let it fall to the floor. With a practiced hand, she unclasped my bra and let it just sit pressed against my breasts. With a stiffened tongue, she slowly pushed it off, slowly revealing the large firmness.

"Oh these are amazing," she breathed with a delighted grin.

Her fingers felt so soft and gentle as she caressed the outer curves. My nipples were already tightening under her touch, but when her thumbs grazed against them, they stiffened even more.

"Mmmm, very responsive, I like that…"

Her mouth was warm and soft and wet when she closed her lips around one tight little peak. I arched my back into her as she lightly pinched the other one. I stroked her silky blonde hair as she teased from one to the other, her tongue or fingers always on both of them.

Athena kept sucking and licking back and forth, and I hardly noticed that her hands had slipped to the fly of my jeans. Before I realized what had happened, she had unbuttoned and unzipped my pants.

She held them open and away from my body. When I glanced down, I was grateful that I always kept myself groomed and that I wore semi-sexy panties that day. They were white silk bikinis to match the bra that was lying around somewhere.

Her tongue tickled as it grazed just inside the waistband of my panties. She exhaled warmly on my lower belly and slowly inched my jeans downward. I lifted my ass up and wriggled my hips to help. She giggled while she tugged firmly. I slipped my feet out of my sandals and everything ended up in a puddle somewhere.

When she stood back up, she slowly removed her own tee shirt and leggings. Her young skin was smooth and taut, and the black bra and panties stood out beautifully against her creamy pale skin. She slid back up to straddle my bare thighs, this time with nothing but a thin piece of satin between her pussy and my leg.

I could feel the wetness and the heat as she ground herself against me. She leaned lithe little body forward until her satin-covered breasts were pressed against mine. They felt firm but pliable. I had never touched any other breasts except my own, and I wanted to feel hers.

"Go ahead," she whispered.

I fumbled a little with the clasp on her bra but it finally released, and I tossed it to the floor with the rest of our clothes. Her small tits were smooth and perky with tiny rosebud peaks in the middle. She took one of my hands and pressed it against one of her breasts. With a small moan, she pressed her fingers against mine, gripping her own flesh with my hand.

As soon as she released my hand, I released her breast. Her face fell until I wrapped my arms around her waist and pulled her closer to me. I cupped both of her tits with my hands and kneaded them softly. When the tiny rosebuds stiffened at my touch, I bent my head to them.

With a light flick, I teased one nipple. She gasped, and I was emboldened. I pinched one lightly with my fingertips, as she had done mine, and then closed my mouth around the other. It felt firm and slightly rubbery, and when I rubbed the tip with my tongue, she moaned loudly.

"Yessssssss," she hissed.

I pinched and licked them both, back and forth, until her hips could not stay still. She was wriggling and gyrating against my thigh hard. I loved the way her body moved against mine and the way she responded to my touch.

"Oh I can't take it," she moaned.

Her body melted between my thighs, and she was kneeling on the floor again. This time, she licked her way up one of my thighs and down the other. Her hot wet tongue and light breath made me gasp and moan like I had never done before. When she pressed her pursed lips against my panties, I gasped loudly. I did not even realize how wet I was until she pressed my juices against my own flesh.

Athena hooked her thumbs inside my panties and slowly dragged them down my legs. My pussy tightened at the sudden cool air, but her warm mouth chased that away instantly. She pressed her lips against me, pushing my thighs further apart with her palms.

She kissed all over, teasing me and tormenting me. I could not even remember the last time anyone went down on me, but suddenly I needed it more than I needed oxygen.

Her tongue finally slipped inside the outer lips to find my swollen clit. It throbbed with desire and when she lightly grazed it, I thought I was going to faint. My chest felt hot, my cheeks were flushed, and my breath was ragged.

"Athena," I whispered.

With nothing else as encouragement, she trapped my aching nub between her lips and flicked her tongue hard and fast over the taut surface. I buried my fingers in her long hair and pulled her face to my body. As she rubbed my clit with her tongue, she slid two fingers deep inside my pussy. She pressed firmly against a place I was not aware of until that moment, and I exploded. My whole body tightened and shuddered, and I writhed on the couch, pulling her face tightly against me. As my climax ebbed, she eased me back down to reality. When she finally looked up at me, she had a glossy grin across those perfect pink lips.

She stood and yanked off her own panties before straddling my lap again.

"Athena? How do I please you? I want to make you feel the way you made me feel…" I was nervous but so desperately wanted to give her the same.

I could feel her slippery wetness against my skin as she pressed her pussy into my thigh. She was thrusting against me, willing her own body towards the edge.

"No, no, not like that," I tried to get her to stop.

Her body stopped moving, and the frustration was evident on her face.

"What? Please, Laura, I need…"

"I know, I want to give it to you."

"You don't have to, I understand all of this is new…"

I wrapped one arm around her slender waist and pulled her down to kiss her. She tasted like my pussy, and our tongues danced to share the sweetness. Her kiss was hungry and demanding, her need evident as it radiated from her body. She kissed me as though her relief was on my lips. As I kissed her back, distracting her by nipping at her bottom lip, I slipped one hand between our bodies to find the source of her desire.

Her sweet little pussy was slippery and hot. My fingers slid over the warmth of her skin, and she gasped loudly, arching her back away from my kiss.

"Oh God, yes, Laura, yes" she groaned, almost painfully.

"Like that?" I let my fingers search and explore her body.

"Oh, almost, right… there…"

Her little clit was swollen, and I knew I had found it when she bucked on my thighs.

"Yes, there," she gasped, "please, there."

I rubbed hard little circles right there, right on the place that made her face taut with need. Her body was tight and almost humming as she got closer and closer. It was breathtaking to watch as my fingers drew out each pleasure from her. I slid my middle finger deep inside her and found what she must have found inside me. When I grazed that spot, she stiffened and held her breath. I twisted my hand around until I could reach that fleshy spot inside as well as her clit. When I rubbed both of them together, she screamed and bucked hard against my hand, digging her nails into my shoulders for balance.

I could feel the slipperiness of her climax dripping down my hand, and I wanted to taste it. I wanted to make her make that face again, that look that was partially surprise, a little shock, and complete pleasure. I just kept rubbing until her body went slack against me.

She finally collapsed on my chest, and I slowly withdrew my hand. She nuzzled my neck and kissed the spot where my own pulse still pounded with delight from watching her.

"Athena, that was amazing," I whispered in her ear.

She giggled, "That's what I'm supposed to say."

After a short recovery (women are fabulous that way I now realize), we curled up together on the couch, and she pulled a blanket over our mutual nakedness. We ended up drifting off to sleep that way, still entwined and entangled on her couch. The combined scents of our fun permeated my senses, and I had the most wonderfully wicked dreams of her.

****

I did end up spending the entire night at her place, and even the next day. One thing to note about sleeping woman to woman is that recovery is much quicker. The first time we dozed off it was only for a few hours. When we woke, she was ready for more and I was in no mood to say no.

With a sexy, breathy voice, she slowly walked me through my next step. The first time my tongue tasted her pussy, I was hooked. It was almost too sexy to believe, hearing her voice describe what she wanted me to do as I did it. It's like she was torn between wanting to help instruct me and wanting to just enjoy it. When she came with my mouth wrapped around her pussy, I felt like the sexiest woman on earth.

After that eye-opening weekend, I ended up spending quite a bit of time with Athena over the next several months. She was so amazing and patient as I navigated my first relationship with a woman. She even understood my hesitation in telling anyone, especially my daughter Chelsea. And we spent half our time together having sex. In her bed, in my bed, in the restaurant, in the bar. She also introduced me to some of her friends so I could get to know some other lesbians.

In a friendly way, we ended up going our separate ways. She found someone who was more ready than I was, and she told me I needed to play the field for a while.

I laughed at her when she said that, "At my age? That's ridiculous."

She just stroked my cheek, "Well, in the world of lesbians, you're new and young and ready to have fun. It had nothing to do with age."

She did have a point, and once I thought it through, I did take her advice. I started dating again, after so many years off the market, but not one single date was with a man.

After about a year or so after that first night, I did end up telling my daughter. The last thing I ever wanted was to have her find out some other way. To her credit, she was amazingly supportive. Apparently, she had a lot of gay friends in college and had started to suspect something anyway. I asked her what she meant, and she just laughed.

"There are only two reasons a woman walks around glowing like that, Mom, and I was pretty sure you weren't pregnant. I just want you to be happy, Mom."

I wrapped her in a hug.

"But can I please be there when you tell Dad?"

I laughed and swatted her away, relishing the thought myself.

A Horny Schoolgirls

On a fall-like Friday night, blonde Maddie celebrated her eighteenth birthday. She had invited her slightly older school friends who had come to visit with ten. They were busy talking to them in a large circle in the living room. The sweet wine flowed generously and there was music in the background. The girls had huge discussions about anything and everything that involved a lot of laughter. It was fun and the girls drank well. Suddenly the conversation was about two women who were lesbians and had been living together for quite some time. Loud cheering came through the room and everyone had a rough remark about it, after which they all laughed. "Would you dare?" One of the schoolgirls in the group cast. Everyone screamed loudly and there were disapproving cries. "I do!" Cried the cheeky Laura. "I only use my middle finger and let her part through the entire room! Then I walk away and then she finds out! "All the girls roared with laughter and never recovered. Laura was a slender girl with dark brown hair that she had neatly cut into a half-length page haircut that made her look a bit drowsy, but in reality, she was very confident.

"Oh, how filthy!" Said elegant Kaylee, "That's nothing for me!" Kaylee was a super slim girl with short blond hair who had already been taken by many boys and she was looking for a new friend again. But to let a girl feel herself, that was too bad for her! "Then tell me about your last conquests, Kaylee!" Shouted long-haired Maddie. Decent Kaylee told about her last friend with whom she had lived wonderfully but who had put her aside after three weeks. The other girls listened jealously and with the water in their mouth, they tried to elicit all sorts of details. After some insistence, Kaylee told about the difficult widening of her legs, making a moaning sound as an illustration and the deep penetration that followed, after which there were loud cheers. With two hands, she indicated the length of the boy's rod and especially the detail that she always said when pulling off "Kaylee! Kaylee! Kaylee! "Had to shout to bring the boy to its peak, the other girls were mouth-watering. But soon, the conversation went somewhere else and the girls laughed crookedly about all the nonsense that came up. It was very late in the evening before everyone got on the bike again, half-drunk to go home. They cheered cheerfully across the dark street to say hello to each other and drove away in small groups.

Kaylee and Laura cycled along for a while because they had to go the same way.

"Did you really mean that dirty lesbian thing?" Kaylee asked Laura.

"Yes, of course, you must have tried everything once," Laura joked.

Kaylee was disgusted, but she was also very curious.

"Who would you dare then?" She asked.

"Well, with blonde Maddie or with horny Katie, I don't know."

"Oooh," said Kaylee relieved, "Fortunately, I don't belong!"

"Well, I don't know, but I dreamed about it sometimes," Laura provoked her.

Kaylee's breath caught. "What? With me?"

"It's just a bit of fingering, you know!" Laura joked back.

"Oooh, Laura! Bahhh! "Kaylee disgusted.

While cycling and half-drunk, she thought feverishly: when she went to bed with a boy, that stiff pole sometimes hurt her, what harm could It be If she let a girl feel herself? And no children could come of it either! And before she knew it, she blurted out: "Tomorrow is Saturday and then I'll be home alone, then you will come to me at eleven o'clock, but I find it very nasty, you know!" Then the girls called each other goodbye and they each cycled home in their own direction.

That night, Laura was lying half-drunk in her bed. She was deeply jealous of tough Kaylee because she dared to go to bed with every boy she encountered, even though she hadn't got any further than to let a girlfriend feel herself. That's why she wanted to experience something intimate with the rugged, brave girl. But wasn't a lesbian encounter too much of a good thing? But Kaylee also lay in bed with mixed feelings. Her weak point was that she could not resist someone who wanted something with her, which is why she went to bed with all those boys. Even when Laura provoked her, she had already gone for it, even though she wasn't even a lesbian! She regretted the insane appointment she had made with the foolish brunette. She just hoped it didn't go and finally fell asleep.

The next day Laura came to visit slender Kaylee. They drank coffee and talked about cows and calves. They both doubted a bit about whether they should start the big adventure. Decent Kaylee was dressed very fashionably in a half-length skirt and a matching blouse that dressed her very slim. Laura, on the other hand, was wearing a flimsy cotton red checkered shirt and dark blue jeans in which her sturdy buttocks worked very well. But together with her neatly cut page hairstyle, she made a sporty impression.

"Do you still dare?" Laura asked uncertainly.

"If you dare, I want to know what you can do," boasted Kaylee.

"I dare!" Bluffed Laura with a trembling voice.

"Then let's go to my bedroom!" Said the pretty blonde.

The girls went to Kaylee's bedroom together. Then they could not ignore it anymore and they were shivering with tension facing each other. Carefully Laura put her hands around Kaylee's slender hips while Kaylee laid her hands on Laura's shoulders. They stood against each other and their heads moved side by side so that they didn't have to look at each other. Oh, how creepy that was! They pulled each other's bodies against them and an incredible feeling of disgust overwhelmed them. "Oooh, this is so gross!" The girls cried. With both hands, they started stroking each other's bodies and the shaking Kaylee got a rough feeling of repulsion. "Do we really have to kiss?" Kaylee asked shivering. "Yes, of course, because otherwise, we won't get any further," Laura said in a trembling voice. She kissed the slender blonde on her slender neck. Kaylee winced but recovered quickly and then she quickly kissed the brunette with the page hairstyle on her neck.

"Oooh, how gross! What is that gross! "She thought. With both hands, they started stroking each other's body again and the shaking Kaylee got a rough feeling of disgust while simultaneously noticing that her breasts were stiff. Laura also felt her breasts swell despite the horror. At the same time, she noticed that the vibrating Kaylee was breathing deeply and panting and she felt her stiff nipples against her. Carefully they kissed each other on the mouth, but that didn't taste really good — another kiss on the mouth. Kaylee was disgusted but stuck. The supple schoolgirls stroked each other's backs and shoulders again and experienced a deeply uncomfortable feeling that they could not bring home.

Suddenly Kaylee felt Laura's hands grabbing her stiff breasts. The firm fingers gently molded her swelling breasts and suddenly Kaylee began to enjoy like never before. All kinds of intimate feelings flowed through her body, making her lesbian from one moment to the next. "Oooh, Laura!" She gasped. They fell into each other's arms again, turned their heads crookedly and opened their mouths. Their lips closed around each other and their tongues bravely slid out and they started an incredibly horny kiss. "Oooh, how horny!" Thought blonde Kaylee, "What a nice lesbian girl!" Laura sucked on Kaylee's lips and fanatically pursued the slender blonde's mouth. "Oooh, what a wonderful blonde girl!" Flashed through her head. She inhaled deeply and sucked Kaylee's lungs, and then she breathed out again and blew Kaylee's lungs full. Kaylee immediately participated and without knowing that it should be that way in a professional lesbian relationship, one sucked the lungs of the other, after which the other sucked himself again with the breath of the other. They ventilated each other deeper and deeper until they saw stars In front of them. Kaylee lowered a hand and kneaded in Laura's jeans that began to moan softly. For a moment, the mouths came apart: "Oooh Laura! You made me a lesbian! "Kaylee gasped." Oooh Kaylee! I am totally lesbian because you are always fucking with all those guys! "Finally, the high word was out and Kaylee flowed with love when she heard that.

They undressed hurriedly and the clothes flew through the bedroom until they were completely naked. The horny girls fell into each other's arms again and began to kiss again passionately. Suddenly Kaylee felt Laura's winding finger between her labia. Oooh, how delicious that was! What could that rough girl finger nice! Kaylee began to flow and in turn lowered her hand and placed it on Laura's soft spot. The pubic hair parted and her hand stroked a large open wound that only leaked love out. Her middle finger curled up and she let the bitch enjoy the intimate caresses. They lowered themselves on the bed until they were lying next to each other, slurpingly kissing each other while they were fingering each other intimately. Kaylee stroked the most sensitive place she could find and heard the girl come panting. Suddenly Kaylee wanted to do something very intimate with the horny bitch. She stood up until she sat on her hands and knees beside Laura. "Oh Laura, I want to taste your love!" She gasped. She turned so that her face was above Laura's lower body. Laura immediately opened her legs to willingly undergo the upcoming treatment. She put her arms above her head as a sign of complete surrender. "Yes! Yes! Kaylee! Do it! "Kaylee leaned over the spread legs of the brown-haired bitch. She saw her labia open and the space between them was filled with a red fleshy mass with a hole in the middle. Kaylee lowered her head as she held out her tongue as far as possible. Her long tongue came right into the damp hole and sank deep into it. She heard Laura screaming with pleasure and felt her legs farther apart. Something smashed into her face. She raised her head and then lowered it again with her tongue out. Again her tongue entered the hole where defenseless Laura screamed with pleasure again. She felt the warm flesh against her lips and a squirt of juice spewed into her mouth. Then Kaylee circled her tongue through the hole that quickly grew and Laura elicited a screech associated with a continuous orgasm. Blonde Kaylee started slurping passionately during tongues because she had come to love the beautiful girl very much.

With both arms defenseless above the head, the brunette writhed wildly through the bed, but Kaylee did not let her escape and remained mercilessly in the horny love hole that was now wide open. She completely indulged in licking the blooming carnation of the defenseless girl who was lying beneath her and as a reward, a delicious sweet juice spewed into her mouth. As she screamed and moaned, she felt the pulsing flower open and close, with a heavy sour lady air-breathing in her face. She gulped up the juice that gushed out. Squirming Laura, screaming, grabbed Kaylee's thighs to give her orgasms a way out and pulled the blonde toward her. Kaylee moved her lower body toward Laura and lifted one leg over her head until she lay on her in a professional sixty-nine position. Wild with horniness, Laura put her arms around Kaylee's lower body and she drove her tongue between the open labia of the horny girl. She wildly licked in Kaylee's craving to rid her own continuous orgasm. Now Kaylee moaned while her third armpit was leaking so much juice that Laura was flooded. The slender girl eagerly lay in Laura's mouth, almost fainting with pleasure. The soft tongue of Laura slid through the wide slit of Kaylee and spun circles around the swollen kitten. Kaylee completely surrendered to the rugged girl lying under her and screamed during her, orgasms her mouth full of the sweet juice that spontaneously flowed from her womb. The schoolgirls were crazy about each other and the pleasure of orgasms seemed to come to an end. The spoiled scent of their horniness drifted through the room, but for both girls, it was an ultimate love scent that only evoked more pleasure.

Fifteen minutes later, they were exhausted in bed, but it didn't take long before they started testing each other's bodies again. Oh, how strong those girls were! Their powerful young bodies moved actively through the bed and did not know when to stop. One time Kaylee was upstairs and the other time Laura. The girls stayed in bed all day long to satisfy each other with their mouths. For hours they were making love and getting ready with their juices becoming ever sweeter and their scents becoming more acidic. Then the fingers and tongues slid into all openings of the body to test each other in the lesbian love game. And each time, they saturated each other with a tidal wave of sweet sticky nectar that they let flow from their fragrant flower.

By the end of the afternoon, they were finally satisfied and awoke from their love rush. They lay in the soaked bed for a moment to relax and discussed the nastiest sex they would have together next time. It was already late and it was time for Laura to go home. They took a shower together to wash away all the juices and odors. They exchanged panties and in love, they gave each other one last sparkling tongue kiss. Moments later, the exhausted Laura with a giant swollen carnation got back on the bike to go home. Oh, how strange it felt; it looked like she had a child!

A Family Gathering

The doorbell rings followed by an overjoyed squeal. Pam skipped her way over to the door and swung it open to see her sister, Stephanie, beaming back at her with equaled excitement. Both were as happy as schoolgirls to see each other after so long apart. When Pam learned her sister was back in town from school, she had to get her to come over and see the new home she and her husband Matt just recently purchased. Matt, however, was far more thrilled to see his wife and his sister-in-law reunite, but for very different reasons.

"I'm so excited to see you back here!" said Pam with glee. "Come inside and meet my husband!"

Matt sat at the couch in the living room and just smirked as he stood to greet Stephanie. "Well hello there. Nice to finally meet you," he said as he held out his hand.

Stephanie just shook her head and pushed it aside to give him a big hug instead. "We greet family more intimately than a handshake," she said to him.

Matt chuckled and nodded. "Well, I can believe that, knowing Pam." Stephanie just gave him a wrinkled nosed smile as she walked with Pam to the kitchen. Matt watched the two girls as they carried on the conversation without him. Despite being six foot four, Matt's quiet nature always showed on his sleeve as he seemed to effortlessly fade out of view from the women. He breathed out nervously and twiddled his thumbs before disappearing to his bedroom for a brief time.

"Don't mind Matt, he can be a bit socially awkward on first meetings," said Pam to her sister. "He really is very sweet and super intelligent. I feel like you two could have a good relationship."

"Well he's your husband, so that would have to be a friendship," chuckled Stephanie quietly. "But I will admit he is very cute. In like an intense sort of way."

"Ladies," interjected Matt as he already crept back up to the girls without them noticing. Stephanie gasped in surprise that he might have heard her and laughed awkwardly as Pam smiled at her husband. "I thought we might enjoy a little game before dinner. I took the liberty to pull one out from our closet that we can play."

"We had board games in the closet?" asked Pam curiously as both women walked with Matt back to the living room couch where they sat down. Pam sat between her husband and sister.

"Not quite like a board game," chuckled Matt as he pulled out a small box. "I call it scratching my curiosity itch." Both girls looked at Matt curiously, even Pam being unsure what he meant by that. Matt lifted from the small box a coin-shaped pendulum as he proceeded to flick it with his finger so it would both rotate and swing back and forth on his hand.

"What is that?" inquired Pam as she squinted at the pendulum shaking. Both her and Stephanie stared at it curiously until they grew silent and steadied their breathing rhymical with the sway of the pendulum. Matt watched their eye movements as they seemed to become immediately entranced by the small silver object.

"Stephanie and Pam," started Matt in a soft-spoken voice. "Close your eyes." Both women closed their eyes on command. Matt looked at them curiously as the pendulum still waved slowly. He breathed out and smirked deviously. "Now open them." They did just that. Their eyes stared at the pendulum blankly. Matt gagged on his excitement as he wasn't sure his plan would work, much less work this well. He thought for a moment how he could prove they really were hypnotized by the magic device. "Throw your arms up in the air." Both of them did just that, throwing up their arms and holding them high up over their heads, the same blank look on their faces.

Matt laughed and stood up as he stopped swaying the hypnotizing device. He couldn't believe it had worked so simply. Pam would never subject herself to something like holding her hands up in the air so foolishly even if both she and her sister were in on it. They stayed just as they were as he commanded it. He thought for a moment. He remembered he had to make a word to snap them out, or it could eventually wear off.

"Your word to return to this state is and always will be…" he started as he looked around the room only to notice one of the ugly Hawaii décor items Pam bought from a thrift shop. "Pineapple." Matt laughed at himself. "When you hear or read the word pineapple, no matter where you are, you will be subject to obey my every command without question. When I snap my fingers three times, then, and only then, will you break from my spell until I should have you once again. You will not remember a thing that happens when you are under the spell and your mind will reason away whatever it is you were doing that seemed out of place."

Now, all Matt needed to do was test if it worked. He breathed out and put the device away. He snapped his fingers three times. Both women stretched their arms more as if they were in mid stretched. "Mmm, your back feeling a bit still too?" asked Pam to Stephanie.

"It feels like it," said Stephanie as they both put their arms down and smiled.

Pam looked back up at Matt curiously. "Dear do you want to help me get dinner ready?"

Matt nodded and looked at the women. "Pineapple," he said plainly. Suddenly both of them returned to a stoic stance. Matt nearly jumped for joy. He still couldn't fully believe it, but now he was sure he'd be able to get away with something a bit more risqué. He breathed out slowly and nodded. "Why don't you two kiss? Show how much you love each other." Pam nodded and turned to Stephanie as they both leaned into each other slowly and kissed on the lips pleasantly. "No no, I mean really kiss. Like you want to fuck!" said Matt extremely excited.

Pam moaned a bit like she was really excited to hear Matt talk dirty. The girls continued to kiss each other with slow, seductive lip movements. Stephanie was the bigger go-getter of the two, as it showed in her kissing. She pushed more into Pam's face and stuck her tongue in her sister's mouth before she is received with the same. Matt licked his lips in delight as he stared at the two women kissing. He felt his member growing in his pants from the steamy sight. He loved Pam, but he loved the idea of Pam having incestual lesbian relationships with her sexy sister more.

Matt's wife had brown hair with beautiful eyes like a multi-colored green and brown hue. In the light, her stare was like a rainbow of color. She was pale and petite compared to her sister who was a perfect contrast. Stephanie had darker hair and deep brown eyes with a naturally tan skin tone. She had a more top-heavy figure compared to Pam that Matt found very attractive in person just like in the pictures. He couldn't have been more excited to see them kissing now.

"Stephanie, you should take your shirt off and let your wonderful breasts breathe. Pam, you never helped your sister out of her clothes from coming over," said Matt. Stephanie nodded and pulled back as she reached around the bottom lining of her shirt and gradually pulled it up over her body. Pam held out her hands to help pull her sister's shirt off as Matt watched her body slowly reveal itself to him. Stephanie's breasts were larger than Pam's, and each fit perfectly in her palms. Pam grasped Stephanie's breasts and pulled up her bra. Matt nearly gagged again at the sight of Stephanie's beautiful, dark, round nipples. The cooler air in the room immediately made them tight and pointy. "Pam, your sister's nipples look cold. Warm them up with your mouth. Suck on them for her."

Pam nodded obediently as she leaned in and pursed her lips on her sister's perky nipples. Stephanie breathed out uncontrollably from the sensitive pleasure. Pam slowly started to suck hard on Stephanie's tits and moan herself from enjoyment. Both women sat there on the couch enjoying the experience as Matt pulled out his thick cock. He breathed out in exasperation as he couldn't help but stroke himself at the sight of the lewd act.

"Now Stephanie, do the same to Pam. Help her out of her clothes and suck on her pretty little pink nipples." Stephanie obeyed and did the same to her sister. Pam's breasts were a lot smaller and she rarely wore a bra in the house. Stephanie leaned in and took Pam's tiny hard nipples into her mouth as she sucked and nibbled on them graciously. Matt watched with an intense stare as he trained his eyes heavily on Stephanie's topless body as her mouth played with his wife's tits.

"That is wonderful. Now both of you, stand," he commanded. The women stopped what they were doing and slowly rose from their seat at the couch. Matt smirked and nodded. "Good girls. Now then, completely undress, both of you." The women both nodded as they undid the buttons of their pants. Matt licked his lips and slowly sat down as he watched Stephanie and Pam both pull their pants and underwear down together, revealing their perfect muffs to him. He breathed out as he carefully examined Stephanie's landing strip pubic hair that perfectly formed luscious pussy lips. It was a nice contrast to Pam's completely shaved albeit beautiful pussy. The women stepped out of their pants in unison and kicked off their heels so they were completely naked.

"Beautiful still," said Matt as he stroked his cock and sat back holding it out to them. "Why don't you two come share giving me head."

Pam nodded obediently as did Stephanie and they both dropped to their knees before Matt. He looked at them in surprised excitement as he was more than ready for this moment. He presented his hard cock to them as both girls came in on both sides of him to lick his shaft. Stephanie on his left and Pam on his right. Matt groaned as he felt their tongues move up and down his cock in opposite directions. He watched as their wet tongues caressed his rigid shaft and the girls moaned in unison. Matt knew that because this worked so well, he not only wanted to savor the moment but wanted to anticipate others far in advance. His wife and his sister-in-law were under his complete control.

Stephanie was first to take initiative and pull his whole cock into her mouth. She dived all the way in and gagged herself on the back of her throat with Matt's thick meat and he was surprised she had that kind of control in her. Stephanie took his cock deep for several long, hard sucks before popping it out of her mouth and handing it to Pam. Pam took it graciously and deep throated as well, something Matt already knew her to be well trained to do, though it was something he always wished she would do more often. Matt clenched his hips and thrusted forward more into Pam, as the sensational overload was getting harder to resist. "Enough," he commanded as he gasped for a breath. The two girls stopped and sat up straight. "Now I want you to fuck each other until you cum."

The girls looked at each other and immediately got into it. They embraced each other and laid out on the floor as Matt watched. He stroked his sensitive wet cock as his eyes widened to see Pam taking more initiative than Stephanie at first. Pam licked her sister's tits and rubbed her hands between her legs. Stephanie moaned and groped her back, rubbing her married sister's clit with her wet fingers. The girls ground their bodies against each other, rubbing their wet lips and clip against each other's legs as they sucked and fingered on each other. Pam pushed her fingers up deep inside Stephanie's cunt and vigorously thrusted to make her sister cum. Stephanie yelped and howled in pleasure as she writhed against Pam's fingers. Pam then pushed her sister back and got down between her legs to suck on her hot clit, wanting to fulfill her duties to make her sister cum with the hypnotic hold still on her. Matt was impressed at how dirty a gay slut his wife could be.

Pam viciously went into her sister's cunt, licking and dipping her tongue in deep within her walls. Stephanie was howling within a minute and shaking her body like a convulsion. Matt groaned as he jerked off harder at the intense scene. Pam had Stephanie arching her back and orgasming so hard she came on Pam's face. "Sweet Jesus," said Matt as he groaned stroking his cock harder at the sight. Stephanie pushed Pam back breathing wildly as she returned the favor, going down on her sister's cunt like it was a pie-eating contest. Pam was moaning and groaning heavily as she was already so close. She whined and whimpered with pleasure as Stephanie wasn't as skilled at a fast orgasm as Pam seemed to be. Stephanie sucked her hard clit and fingered her wet hole until Pam started to howl just as she did. "Oh fuck," said Matt as he stood up. He stumbled over to Pam and got on his knees. "Drink me dry my dear!"

Pam writhed against Stephanie's tongue deep in her hole as her whole body arched to ride against her sister's face. Matt jerked his cock to orgasm as he moaned and placed it in Pam's mouth. Path moaned on his sensitive head as it exploded inside her mouth. She sucked it down slowly, drinking up Matt's cum without complaint. Matt shook from the ecstasy and happy to finally have made his wife eat his seed. He rubbed out the last few drops before pulling away and breathing out heavily. "All right, you may stop. Take a moment to clean yourselves and put your clothes back on," he said as he put his cock away. Matt took a seat and watched patiently as the women moved like zombies to the bathroom to clean up then back to where their clothes were to redress. Matt waited until they appeared completely redressed as they were. He breathed out nervously, thinking his command for them to not remember wouldn't work this time. "You may sit back down as you were, ladies."

Pam and Stephanie both sat back down on the couch as Matt sat up where he was seated and snapped his fingers. "So… wait," Pam paused. "What were we talking about?" She looked at Stephanie curiously then to Matt as she smacked her lips. "My mouth feels weird all of a sudden."

"That is because you're hungry, and we were about to start cooking," said Matt as he stood up casually.

Stephanie rubbed her head curiously, wincing like she had a headache. "I am hungry," she said. "I guess I didn't realize how long its been since I ate this morning. Feeling light-headed myself."

Matt looked at the girls curiously and smirked. "Maybe some wine will help? I'll get the wine!" He whisked himself away into the kitchen as the girls looked at him curiously, both being none the wiser.

The next day came as Stephanie was out in the city, having stayed the night with Matt and Pam since she was only in town to visit for a few days. She was out clothes shopping while Matt and Pam were at work. Her phone ringed with a text and she quickly checked it while in the middle browsing a rack of clothes thinking nothing of the night before. She pulled up the message from Matt. "See if you can find Pam a pineapple dress," Matt said in the text. Stephanie read the trigger word and immediately paused what she was doing. A second text popped up. "Send a picture of yourself in the store you're at."

Stephanie nodded reading the message as she didn't seem to react or think that Matt's messages were odd. She held the phone out and smiled into it getting one of the signs behind her displaying the name of the store. She sent the text to Matt and waited like a servant waiting for their master's orders. Another message popped up. "Thank you. Why don't you show me what you're wearing in the dressing room mirror?" Stephanie nodded and walked over to the dressing room where she held out her phone and took a shot of herself smiling for Matt. A few people walked by her out of the dressing room, looking at her curiously wondering what she might be doing. Stephanie looked back down at the phone as the next message came up. "Take your underwear off where no one can see you and walk around the store while you masturbate. Don't get caught, but do put me on video."

Stephanie looked around making sure she isn't seen as she walks into one of the dressing rooms. She calls Matt on video and he answers with a quiet smirk. He watched as Stephanie set the phone down and pulled up her skirt. She slid her underwear down off her legs and balled them up to put in her purse. She then held her leg up so Matt could see her full pussy lips as she rubbed her fingers a few times over it. Matt breathed out and sat back at his desk where he had full privacy inside his office. He pulled out his cock and proceeded to masturbate behind the desk watching Stephanie. Stephanie gave him a light moan as she then pulled her skirt down and grabbed up the phone. She kept it close to her chest so Matt could see her cleavage as she walked out of the dressing room and back into the store.

Stephanie approached a rack of clothes and situated herself against it and lowered the phone. Matt watched as she slipped her fingers over her pussy and made sure she was nice and wet as she teased her hole. Matt quivered at the thought, feeling the sense of danger in her being caught to be even more thrilling than the idea that the girls would remember what he made them do. He was fully aware of one of the side effects of the hypnotism, that the acts performed under hypnosis will slowly come to be a part of the person committing them internally if done with repetition. He wanted to make Stephanie his special side whore that he could share with his wife, perhaps one day on their own volition.

He watched Stephanie as she moved around to all different parts of the store, showing how many people are around her before showing her wet pussy to the phone camera and masturbating for several seconds on in. She eventually came in a long stream of hot wet fluid while sitting in the back area of the Men's shoe section which was completely empty. Matt groaned as he watched her cum all along her leg in her skirt as he came on the floor under his desk. He sat back and breathed out excited. "Beautiful. You may continue your day as normal now, but I want you to be thinking about me and Pam and all the ways you can please us later." He chuckled, wondering if that command would work as he hung up to leave Stephanie in the wind.

Pam was working diligently at the restaurant she managed when she received a text from Matt. She paused to check the message he sent to her. "Serving any pineapple tonight?" he asked. Pam paused and looked at the message as she was put in her trance. "I want you, babe. Send me a picture of some of the food you have there on your tits. Do it discreetly."

Pam looked around curiously at everyone in the back working to get the food served. She grabbed a dessert plate of strawberry shortcake and quickly made her way to the bathroom. She breathed heavily with the excitement of fulfilling her master's desires. She checked to make sure no one was coming into the bathroom and locked the door. She popped her breasts out of her uniform and proceeded to smear the cake and its icing across her tits. She pulled out the phone and took a selfie as she presented her beautiful little pink nipples for Matt to see now decorated in cake crumb and icing spread.

Matt looked at the picture and smirked. He messaged Pam back. "Wonderful choice my love, now take the rest of the cake and decorate your pussy with it. Take a video for me to watch."

Pam nodded as she read the instructions. She grabbed the cake and sat against the counter of the sink. She pulled down her panties and pulled up her work skirt as she took her phone and started filming. She spread her pussy open and proceeded to rub her clit with the cake's icing as lubricant. She moaned for the video as she rubbed her pussy long and delicately, really getting in there. After a moment she stopped and sent the video. She breathed out nervously as there was one more command. "Good girl. Take your underwear all the way off and leave the icing on your body. I want you to get back to work without your underwear. Cover the rest of yourself back up and look none the wiser. Think about how much you're in love with your sister and me and how much you want to fuck me and her when you get home."

Pam read her command and bit her lip as she looked down at the mess. She pulled her panties all the way off and discarded them to stay discreet. She pulled her skirt back down and put her breasts away after cleaning them off and eating the rest of the cake. She tossed the plate and shook her head; her mind attempting to focus and look normal even though she is still in her trance-like state. She walked back outside into the restaurant smiling and looking like nothing was different about her. The feeling of the icing coated on her pussy was ever noticeable. She overheard a customer complaining that they're having to wait too long for their shortcake dessert.

Matt watched the video over a few times looking at the pictures as he smirked. He messaged them to Stephanie with the command. "I want you to masturbate to your sister before we get there. Watch and think about just how hungry she makes you. You want her." He sent the message and smirked deviously as he sat back and sighed. He shrugged as he double-checked that his office was locked and decided to jerk another one out while he had the free time to his wife's pictures.

It was later now in the evening when Matt came home first. He arrived right around the time Pam did. He smiled and gestured for her to come to him. She smiled as she approached him and they kissed. He curiously looked at her as he could tell from her dilated eyes that she was still firmly in her trance despite acting like her usual self otherwise. "Did anyone find out what you did, naughty girl?" asked Matt.

Pam shook her head. "No, I was never caught," she said with a devious little chuckle.

"And are you ready to pounce when your sister comes back?"

"More than ever."

Matt led Pam inside and commanded her to strip to the nude. Pam obeyed as she stood by the open door and stripped down. Matt looked outside to see if any neighbors were peeping and smirked as his wife bared her beautiful white ass to the world then stood there calmly, stark naked. "Put your clothes out of the way then stand here and wait for Stephanie. When she comes in. Show her how much you've missed her."

Matt stepped back and sat himself down as Pam did as she was told, standing back at the door. It was only about five minutes later that the door opened and Stephanie walked in. Before she could say anything, Pam embraced her from behind and grasped her breasts through her clothes. Stephanie immediately moaned and gasped in surprise, having been building up that sexual energy all day for this because of Matt's commands. She turned and grasped her sister by the cheeks and kissed her lips gently. Pam immediately started to undress Stephanie right there in the open door. Matt casually stood up and walked over to close it, spotting one of their neighbors out walking the dog had stopped to stare at the image on display. Matt smirked and waved to them as he closed the door. "Ladies, you'll be more comfortable in the bedroom."

Both Stephanie and Pam couldn't stop giggling as they ran to the bedroom with Matt following behind. Stephanie threw off all of her clothes as she embraced her sister and they laid back hard on the bed making out. Matt undressed as he watched the two girls begin to finger fuck each other and lock tongues while they moaned against each other. He breathed out and stroked his cock. "Let me get involved this time," he insisted. He crawled up on to the bed as the two women sat up and started rubbing their hands over his body and cock.

Pam immediately started sucking on Matt's cock with great vigor as Matt licked lips with Stephanie and grasped her ass firmly in his hand. He thrusted into Pam's mouth as he started playing with Stephanie's ass and pussy from behind. Matt groaned with pleasure as he lightly pulled Pam's hair to move so Stephanie can have a taste. Stephanie breathed out and obeyed as she took Matt's cock in hungrily and sucked on him hard. Matt loved the thought of finally letting Stephanie taste his dick. He watched as he thrusted slowly up into her mouth. Stephanie sucked graciously as Matt directed Pam to get behind her and eat her out. Pam obeyed as she wrapped her hands around Stephanie's waist and licked her tongue up and along her pussy with glee.

Stephanie moaned heavily on Matt's cock as he watched Pam tongue fuck her and finger her wet hole. "Beautiful, now turn around," he demanded as Stephanie nodded and obeyed. "Give your sister the same courtesy."

Pam sat back and spread her legs open as Pam pushed her face down into her wet pussy. She presented her ass to Matt as he licked his lips and rubbed his cock against her lips. He breathed out heavily as he pushed into Stephanie slowly, letting her moan into his wife's cunt. Pam rubbed her clit as Stephanie tongue fucked her hole, moving in motion with Matt as he started to vigorously thrust against her, their bodies slapped together with how fast they moved in motion. Matt leaned his body over Stephanie and grabbed and played with her breasts. He pinched her hard nipples and caressed the soft fullness of her chest as he thrusted deep inside her. Stephanie whimpered and moaned with such pleasure as Matt then reached under and started rubbing her clitoris. He felt Stephanie's body shake against his as he thrusted faster and faster. Stephanie started to cum and ride Matt's dick harder and harder as he groaned in pleasure. Pam rubbed her hair and grabbed it to help push her back on to Matt.

Matt quickly turned Stephanie over on her back and pulled Pam to him. He knew better than to cum inside of his sister-in-law. He pulled Pam on top of Stephanie and made her get to work on riding Stephanie's cunt through her orgasm. Matt pushed himself inside Pam and returned to thrusting. Pam shook with pleasure as she was already so close to orgasming. Stephanie's saliva made Pam's pussy easy to slide in and out of as Matt clinched his wife's ass hard and pounded harder and faster with as much control as he could manage. He gasped in pleasure as Pam climaxed with him. He felt his seed release inside his wife as she rubbed Stephanie off to another large orgasm. The harmonious sounds of their moaning together were a symphony of music to Matt's ears.

After a moment letting everyone ride out their climaxes, Matt slowly pulled away and laid back. "Very good, my sweet ladies," he said. "Both of you, go get cleaned up and dressed. When you're done, we can start dinner. Stephanie, you will want to stay with us for a long time. Just the three of us." Stephanie nodded as both girls got up and went to the shower. Matt thought long and hard about whether or not he would ever snap his fingers again, or see if the hypnotism would slowly take over their lives and make them permanently his without consequences. He wondered if anything hey did would ever be by their own volition again.

"Matt," called Pam from the bathroom. Matt sat up nervously as she sounded like her old self again. "Would you like to come join us, my love?"

"I'll be right there my dear," he called back. Matt's lips curled into a devious smile as he pulled out the box with the pendulum and pulled it out. He held the coin in his hand and kissed it graciously before putting it away and quickly making his way into the bathroom after the girls.

Swapping and Swimming

Angus and Sophia had been in their house for fifteen years. Angus was an avid do-it-yourselfer, and since Sophia was busy with the design and gardens, they had the house in good condition.

Their new neighbor's Bruno and Amelia were younger and they had bought a house at a bargain price that had not changed much since the 1970s. They worked hard to catch up with the furniture and improve their skills.

Many conversations took place over the fence, especially on weekends.

On one Saturday the residents on both sides of the fence were very busy until they stopped at about 5 pm.

Angus' last words were: "Skinny dipping our pool 8 pm sharp".

"You and your big mouth and your strange sense of humor, they may never speak to us again," Sophia lamented.

"Whenever we use our pool, it's usually just after dusk because you like the lights - and we go in naked so we don't have to rinse our bathers or destroy them with the chlorine.

"Yes, but we have no company and we invite them to be naked."

"A quick look at Amelia's tits would be better than a five-star movie."

"They're probably no prettier than mine."

"Probably not, but variety is the spice of life, and it could be detail, firmness, nipple length, colouring or something interesting.

"Angus, I think you're getting worse as you get older."

Around 8pm, Angus and Sophia were swimming naked in their pool and thought it highly unlikely they'd have company - until Bruno and Amelia walked in and had nothing on unless you count the two curled up towels Bruno was wearing.

The visitors ran wildly towards the pool, shouting 'Good evening' as they bombed into the water.

"Do you often have lean dip evenings here," Amelia asked.

"Just us, never in company before, I thought Angus might have offended you, what about you, are you regulars in the nude bathing scene?

"Twice before, when we went to a mixed onsen in Japan, Bruno was disappointed because the ladies had such small tits, even if they were more to his taste, he couldn't have seen them through the steam.

"Another time, we jumped into a pond beside Ben Nevis in Scotland. Although it was the middle of summer, it was so cold that we couldn't find Bruno's penis or my nipples for an age afterwards.

"I have to thank you both for lending me tools, recommending craftsmen and advising me on do-it-yourself," said Amelia.

"Why change the subject, I enjoyed the tits and the nude swimming," Angus said, getting a serious look from Sophia.

They stayed in the water for an hour and Sophia suggested they have coffee on the terrace.

"You both reflect us in some way, the men have a strange sense of humour and we are all quite frank," commented Sophia.

"You can't argue with that," said Amelia, "it feels as if we've known you for years.

"You both, how shall I put it, come over here naked in response to something that could have been a joke, that's very daring, lead an exciting social life," Angus asked.

"Do we get along with other people, is that what you want to say?" asked Bruno.

"That's none of our business, we're just talking," Angus replied, sounding apologetic.

"We have swum naked with other people, two, now three times. Twice we've been to parties that were about gentle swapping. We didn't go back to reach higher levels of swapping.

"I'm curious, what exactly is soft-swapping?"

Partners are swapped to kiss. Normally, on this level, everyone is in the same room. Depending on the group, the rules may allow touching above the waist, under or over the clothes".

"Sounds like harmless fun," Angus said, "I'm ready when the rest of you are ready too.

"I think we must discuss this Angus," Sophia said sternly.

"We've just done that. All those in favour, raise your hand."

Three and a half votes in favor, counting a somewhat weak arm rising from Sophia.

The girls went into the house to freshen up and came back in underpants.

"Topless smooching, here we come," said an excited Bruno.

They started with the men sitting on patio chairs, with one girl on each lap. For greater comfort, they went on couches and lay down horizontally.

Within thirty minutes, they all emerged to get some air. After a very exhausting day they were tired and waking up on a cramped couch would not lead to a productive Sunday.

Amelia asked Sophia how she was feeling.

"I've always been a bit of a prude. A few hours ago I would have divorced Angus because he agreed to a gentle swing, he almost got kicked out because he invited you to swim naked. My attitude changes from minute to minute.

"It has to do with the feeling that we have known you for years and like and respect you both so much that the whole process is accelerated and exciting.

"Now I wonder what would give me more pleasure, a good hard fuck with Bruno or watching Angus fuck Amelia - but not tonight, I'm knackered."

"Well, same time, same place, same order of undress, tomorrow?" Bruno asked.

"Will I see you for coffee sometime during the day to plan the evening?" Angus suggested.

There was a lot of excitement in the air the following day at the morning coffee.

"Shall we swap places after our swim tonight?" Bruno asked.

"Shall we all continue with kissing and touching above the waist? asked Angus.

Four hands were raised very quickly.

"That's the tricky part, do we add oral sex on women, blowjobs, vaginal sex as a gradual process or do we jump ahead with our feet.

"All this," they shouted in unison.

Do we really have to develop a set of rules or do we just have to play it by ear? asked Sophia.

i

"Rule number one for most groups should be No means no. But I cannot imagine that there are insoluble border issues within this group," Amelia noted.

"In some groups, there might be jealousy because a couple only kiss and their spouses are kissing each other, and their spouses are going at it over the top full-gender. That wouldn't apply to us either," said Sophia.

"You know, these deck chairs are not meant for two. Shouldn't the ladies go into the comfort of their own bed and let the men change the house, or is that too bold at the moment? asked Angus.

"I would feel very safe in this situation with my spouse next door. And Sophia, if my husband tries to enter the wrong hole and doesn't take no for an answer, you have my permission to cut his balls off with a plastic spoon. exclaimed Amelia.

"Just kidding, Bruno, I know you'll treat Sophia with the same kindness and respect I get." She went on.

The swimming lesson went on as before, only this time Bruno and Amelia bombed the water and shouted: Rubba Dubba Doo!

The coffee on the terrace was drunk very quickly. Angus and Amelia went next door, Bruno and Sophia went upstairs.

Bruno and Sophia hopped into bed.

Sophia called her husband: "I'm about to pick up another man's cock, the first time since I met you. I love you," said Sophia.

He replied, "We're off to a slow start, but tonight my cock goes in Amelia's mouth and pussy, the first time since we met, it's somewhere else than with you. I love you, sweet dreams."

He hung up the phone and reached for the pussy.

"Oral sex in both directions, me on top, then lots of cuddling and a good night's sleep," Sophia asked.

"Sounds perfect," he replied, "Let me know if you're not feeling well or if you want me to do something special, can't wait to find the most sensitive parts of your pussy lips.

Next door, Angus and Amelia collapsed in armchairs, each with a glass of iced water, to get some rest before the main event. They recovered quickly,

Amelia approached him on her knees with a mouth full of ice. She took his cock in her mouth and used her tongue and swirled the ice and her tongue with great effect.

When enough ice had melted so that she could speak, she said, "I think if this was done properly, it would be alternately hot and cold.

How was that?"

"Incredibly good", and with that he moved her back to her chair and slowly fed ice cubes into her vagina with his tongue.

"How was that?"

"More than amazing."

So, they went upstairs and had Angus-on-top missionary sex and snuggled up until morning.

The next day was a holiday. They all sat around the morning coffee cups and looked, as they say, like cats that had been in the cream.

They agreed to schedule an extra night once a month for their birthdays, holidays, National Windbag Day, St. Patrick's Day, King Solomon's birthday and any other special events that might arise.